"You are here—
Margot is not."

Andreas spoke carefully. "After all," he went on, "Leon is only human. He is not immune to beautiful women."

Sylvie drew an unsteady breath. "If you're suggesting Leon is interested in me...."

"I can tell by the way he looks at you that he finds your company... sympathetic."

Sylvie was trembling. Being with Andreas disturbed her in a way that was essentially dangerous. His presence stimulated her imagination in a manner both thrilling and shocking.

Andreas sensed her agitation without guessing the reason for it. "You can trust Leon," he said. "He is in need of...consolation, that is all. I will speak to him—"

"No!" Sylvie cried, stung by his lack of perception. "Leave me alone. And leave Leon alone, too. He doesn't need you, and neither do I!"

ANNE MATHER
is also the author of these

Harlequin Presents

and these

Harlequin Romances

Many of these titles are available at your local bookseller.

For a free catalogue listing all available Harlequin Romances
and Harlequin Presents, send your name and address to:

HARLEQUIN READER SERVICE
1440 South Priest Drive, Tempe, AZ 85281
Canadian address: Stratford, Ontario N5A 6W2

ANNE MATHER

innocent obsession

Harlequin Books

TORONTO • LONDON • LOS ANGELES • AMSTERDAM
SYDNEY • HAMBURG • PARIS • STOCKHOLM • ATHENS • TOKYO

Harlequin Presents edition published November 1981.
ISBN 0-373-10468-5

Original hardcover edition published in 1981
by Mills & Boon Limited

CHAPTER ONE

'I don't think I can do it, Margot,' said Sylvie carefully, breaking off a spear of celery and biting into its crisp heart. Margot's table was always liberally spread with low-calorie foods, and after a lunch of only cottage cheese and fresh pineapple, Sylvie's healthy young stomach was still far from satisfied.

'Why can't you do it?' her sister demanded impatiently, fairly snatching the bowl of celery out of Sylvie's reach and gazing at her penetratingly. 'What do you plan to do from now until October? Vegetate?'

Sylvie shrugged, causing the corn-gold curtain of her hair to swing forward around her cheeks. 'I was going to try and find a job,' she admitted, reduced to blotting up the crumbs of cottage cheese that still lingered on her plate, and Margot leaned towards her triumphantly, pointed elbows resting on the table.

'There you are, then,' she declared. 'This is a job I'm offering you. Go out to Alasyia, look after Nikos for six weeks. I'll pay you, and I've no doubt Leon wouldn't be averse to——'

'No, Margot.'

'Why not?'

Sylvie shook her head. 'Margot, Leon asked you. Nikos is your child. Don't you want to help your own son?'

Margot's fashionably thin face gained a little unbecoming colour as she sank back in her chair, long, scarlet-tipped nails tapping irritably on the arm. 'Sylvie, you're being unreasonable,' she said, drawing in her breath and expelling it again with emphasis. 'You know perfectly well that I can't leave London at this time. Maurice has just found me this part—and it's a good one. I won't—I simply won't be dictated to by you or anyone else!'

Sylvie tilted her head to one side and considered her reflection in the silver-plated coffee pot. As sisters they weren't very much alike, she acknowledged, without rancour. Margot, nine years her senior, was at least three inches taller, and slender as a reed, while Sylvie's five feet four inches were infinitely more rounded. Margot's hair was silver blonde, and she wore it in a gamine cut that gave her a boyish air, totally belied by slanting green eyes and curling lashes. Sylvie, on the other hand, couldn't afford the expense of a regular trip to the hairdresser, and in consequence, her hair was long and thick, and abysmally straight, and the colour of wheat at harvest time. Still, she reflected, her skin was good, and she tanned quite easily, which Margot never had, and if her looks were only interesting, whereas Margot's were striking, that was only fair when Margot's appearance was so much more important to her.

'I think you should write to Leon,' Sylvie said now, looking across the table at her sister again. 'Explain the situation. Tell him that it's impossible for you to get away at this time. Ask him if there isn't someone else who could take care of Nikos.'

Margot's lips tightened. 'You think it's that simple, don't you?' she demanded. 'You really think if I write to Leon and explain the situation, he'll make other arrangements?'

Sylvie grimaced. 'I don't see why not.'

Margot made an impatient sound. 'You forget, Sylvie, Leon isn't like us. He's not English, he's Greek. And Greek men have an entirely different idea of women from Englishmen.'

'He married you, didn't he?' Sylvie frowned. 'He knew

you were an actress.'

'He knew I was *trying* to be,' retorted Margot shortly. 'I hadn't actually done anything. As a matter of fact, I was desperate. If Lewis hadn't suggested I join his modelling group for that trip, I'd never have met Leon, would I? Never have married him!'

Sylvie absorbed this. Seven years ago, when Margot married Leon Petronides, she had been eleven, and scarcely old enough to understand her sister's situation. All she remembered was Margot's elation when she came home from the modelling trip to Athens, her exuberance at having met Aristotle Petronides' son, and later on, her excitement when Leon followed her to London. The wedding that followed soon afterwards had seemed like a dream come true. Despite his parents' disapproval, Leon had refused to give Margot up, and their honeymoon in Fiji had been the envy of all her friends. It was only as Sylvie grew older, after Margot's son, Nikos, was born, that the flaws in their relationship became evident, and although Margot's life with Leon had seemed idyllic, she had begun to get bored.

Twelve months ago, things had come to a head. After six years of behaving as Leon's parents expected their sons' wives to behave, her own father had died, and as Leon was away at the time on a business trip to the United States, Margot had flown home alone to attend the funeral.

Unfortunately, she had not wanted to go back. Initially, using her mother's grief as an excuse, she had stayed on, sharing the house in Wimbledon with Sylvie and her mother, littering the place with her make-up and perfumes, monopolising the bathroom in the mornings, when Sylvie was trying to get ready for school.

Eventually, of course, she had been unable to resist contacting her agent, Maurice Stockton, and as luck would have it, he had just the part for her, in a play that was about to go on tour. The actress who had originally accepted the role had been taken ill, and Margot had jumped at the chance. She had moved out of the house in Wimbledon, much to her mother's relief, and by the time she returned to London, she had enough money to rent this furnished apartment, in a converted Victorian mansion in Bayswater.

Leon had objected, of course, and Mrs Scott, Sylvie's mother, had tried to placate him on those occasions when he had rung the house; but she found it hard to be convincing when she objected, too, and was alternately worried about her grandson and the precarious state of her elder daughter's marriage.

At Easter, Leon had come to London to take his wife home, only to find her embroiled in rehearsals for a new play. He had ranted and raved, but Margot had been all-appealing, all-persuasive, earning herself a further three months' grace. But now, Leon was adamant. Margot must come home—not least, because the nursemaid who had taken care of Nikos since his babyhood was leaving to care for her sick mother.

'Anyway,' Margot went on now, 'Leon won't listen to me. Don't you think I've tried? It's that family of his, of course. They've put him up to it. Without their interference, I could probably have wheedled another six months out of him, but——'

'What about your son?' Sylvie broke in protestingly. 'It's almost a year since you saw him. Don't you care about him at all?'

Margot assumed a brooding expression. 'Of course I care,' she retorted sharply. 'But I'm an actress, Sylvie. I have a career, and to succeed in any profession you have to be dedicated.'

'Then get a divorce,' declared Sylvie practically. 'Tell

Leon the truth. Tell him you don't want to be married to him any longer. You're a British citizen. He can't force you to go back to Greece.'

Margot gave her sister an irritated look. 'I didn't say I didn't want to be married, did I?' she exclaimed, and while Sylvie stared at her incredulously, she continued: 'I—well, I want to do both. Other women do. Other women have both a marriage and a career.'

'Not when their husband lives in Greece, and they live in London,' replied Sylvie crisply. 'Oh, Margot, why won't you be honest? What you really mean is, you don't want to let Leon go because he's a meal ticket, a sure-fire insurance to fall back on, when—*if*—your acting career falls flat!'

'You little prig! Don't you dare to preach to me like that,' Margot declared angrily, her voice rising ominously. 'You know nothing about it. Just because you've got a few academic qualifications, you think you know it all, don't you? Well, you don't. When it comes to the real world, you're sunk! And don't think three years at Oxford will make the slightest bit of difference, because it won't!'

Sylvie sighed, shrugged her shoulders, and rose to her feet, glancing down at her uniform of jeans and tee-shirt without resentment. Margot was probably right. She was only eighteen, after all, and she had just finished her final exams. Going to Oxford was important to her, but she had to admit that compared to Margot's experiences, her own were prosaic. She had never mixed with artistic people, gone on modelling assignments, had handsome men phoning her at all hours of the day and night; and no wealthy Greek was likely to defy his parents and marry her. Nevertheless, she couldn't help thinking that such experiences seemed far more desirable from a distance, than they did close to.

'So you won't help me?' Margot stated, looking up at her with cold accusing eyes, and Sylvie felt a moment's contrition.

'I can't,' she said, wishing she hadn't such a soft conscience. 'I'm sorry, but this is something you're going to have to work out for yourself, Margot.'

'Then I'll ask Mummy,' her sister declared, standing up also, tall and slim and vaguely intimidating, and Sylvie gasped.

'You wouldn't!'

'Oh, I would,' Margot nodded. 'I'm desperate, Sylvie. One way or the other I'm going to do this play, and no one's going to stop me.'

Sylvie sought about for words to dissuade her. 'But— but Mummy would hate it,' she exclaimed. 'She doesn't know Leon's family. Why, she hardly knows Leon himself.'

'I know that.' Margot was unmoved.

'But, Margot, she's just making a life for herself here.' Sylvie spread her hands. 'Since Daddy died, you know how lonely she's been, but now she's joined the Women's Institute, and she plays bridge every Friday—she's even learning to play golf! You can't take her away from all that.'

Margot moved across to the screened fireplace and took a cigarette from the pack lying on the mantel. Lighting it, she said, slowly and deliberately: 'Do you think she would turn her back on Nikos? Do you think she would allow him to be cared for by strangers?'

Sylvie made a sound of impatience. 'That's blackmail, Margot!'

'No, it's not.' Margot swung round, exhaling delicately. 'If you won't help me, there's no one else.'

Sylvie's shoulders hunched. 'Leon will never agree——'

'We won't tell him,' declared Margot dispassionately.

'You will simply arrive in my place——'

'No!'

'No?'

Sylvie's tongue circled her dry lips. 'What will he think? What will he do?'

'You'll convince him that it was impossible for me to leave London at this time,' said Margot relentlessly. 'Leon won't argue—he's too much of a gentleman for that. And by the time he's thought of a way to circumvent my plans, Dora will be back.'

'Dora?'

'The nursemaid. Her mother won't remain sick for ever.'

Sylvie ran troubled fingers up the back of her neck and into the heavy weight of her hair. 'Margot——'

'Well?' Margot's aristocratically thin features were cold. 'Are you going to turn me down?'

Sylvie moved her head helplessly from side to side. 'When are you supposed to leave?'

'Next Tuesday.'

'Tuesday!' Sylvie sounded panic-stricken. 'Margot, I can't be ready to leave by Tuesday.'

'Why not? What do you have to do? Pack a couple of swimsuits, and a dress for the evenings.' Her sister's lips curled. 'Not, I trust, those disgusting denims you're wearing at present. Do you have any idea how tight they are?'

Sylvie broke the news to her mother after dinner that evening.

She was going to a disco with Brian Jennings, and in her uncertain mental state she thought it would be easier if her mother got over the shock while she was not around. But to her astonishment, Mrs Scott's reaction was one of relief, not disapproval.

'I knew Margot was going to ask you,' she said, causing Sylvie to catch her breath in confusion. 'I told her there was no possibility of me going, after promising to help the vicar with the summer youth festival, but I thought you might enjoy it, as we haven't booked a holiday this year.'

Sylvie was dumbfounded. Margot had tricked her. Far from hesitating over asking their mother to take her place, she had actually come to her first, and the threatening tone she had adopted towards Mrs Scott's involvement had been just so much hot air.

'But don't you think Margot is being a little selfish?' she ventured now, as Mrs Scott settled herself in her chair in front of the television set, hoping for an unfavourable reaction, but her mother only shrugged.

'Margot must get this acting bug out of her system,' she declared, flicking through the pages of a television magazine. 'Turn on the set, will you darling? I don't want to miss my serial.'

Sylvie was thoughtful at the disco that evening, and Brian took exception to her silent introspection.

'What's wrong?' he demanded, drawing her into a corner and shielding her from the rest of the gathering with his stocky body. 'Is it something I said, or didn't you want to keep this date or something?'

'No. No.' Sylvie slipped her arms around his neck apologetically, smiling at his angry expression. 'It's just something that happened today, that's all. Something I don't much like—but which I've got to do now, because I promised.'

'What?' Brian was puzzled. 'You didn't agree to go on that dig, did you? I thought you said——'

'It's not the dig,' retorted Sylvie flatly, momentarily dispelling his frown. Mr Hammond, her history tutor, had invited her to join a dig he was organising in Northumberland: but in spite of her interest in antiquity, she had declined, mainly because she had felt the need to get a job, and contribute something to the family budget. Besides, Brian, whose own interests lay in a more technical direction, had objected to her spending several weeks camping up north while he was kicking his heels in London, and she realised his reaction to her proposed trip to Greece was going to be far harder to handle than her mother's.

'As a matter of fact, I am going away,' she said now, distracting his attention from the soft curve of her neck, and Brian drew back.

'Going away?' he echoed. 'You mean—on holiday? But I thought you said——'

'Not on holiday,' Sylvie contradicted with a sigh. 'It's a job really.' She hesitated. 'I'm going to Alasyia to look after Margot's little boy for a few weeks.'

'Alasyia? You mean—Greece, don't you?'

Sylvie nodded.

'I see.' Brian drew back completely, and Sylvie's hands dropped to her sides. 'When was this decided?'

'Just today—I told you.'

Brian looked sceptical. 'You mean—today was the first you heard of it?'

'Well, not exactly. I mean——' Sylvie was finding it difficult to be honest, 'Margot knew about it, of course, and I knew Leon wanted her to go——'

'Leon? That's your brother-in-law, isn't it?'

'Yes.' Sylvie nodded again. 'Anyway, as I was saying, Leon asked Margot to go home, but she's busy with a play at the moment——'

'——so she asked you?'

'Yes.'

'Do you want to go?'

Sylvie grimaced. 'You have to be joking!'

'So why didn't you refuse?'

'I did, at first. But then—oh, Brian! She said she'd ask Mummy, and I thought Mummy would go, and she'd be miserable, so I had to agree.'

Brian's mouth compressed. 'It doesn't matter about me, of course.'

Sylvie sighed. 'Yes, it does—I've told you. I didn't want to go. But now I've promised, so I have to.'

Brian frowned. 'Why doesn't this—Leon employ a nanny?'

'He did. He does. Dora—that's her name—she's had to go and take care of her sick mother——'

'Her sick mother!' Brian was scathing.

'It's true!' Sylvie flushed. 'Can't you try and understand? This isn't easy for me either. Leon expects Margot, and I'm going in her place!'

Brian sniffed. 'For how long?'

'I don't know. Two or three weeks ...' Sylvie was doubtful, but unwilling to mention the six weeks Margot had stipulated.

'Three weeks!' Brian was aggressive. 'That's longer than the dig was going to last!'

'I know it.' Sylvie touched his sleeve tentatively. 'I don't want to go, Brian, honestly.'

Brian's jaw jutted. 'So you say. But what about me? What am I supposed to do for three weeks? Hang about, waiting for you to come back? I'm going to be a laughing stock!'

'No, you're not.' Sylvie wriggled a finger through the buttonhole in his leather jacket. 'Besides,' she ventured a smile, 'aren't I worth waiting for?'

'I don't know, do I?' Brian retorted. 'You haven't let me find out yet!'

Sylvie's colour deepened. 'There's more to a relationship than sex,' she said huskily. 'And I don't sleep around.'

'I'm not asking you to sleep around,' Brian countered, slipping his arms around her waist again and drawing her towards him. 'Only with me.'

'No, Brian.'

'What do you mean? No—now, no—later, or no—for all time?'

Sylvie licked her lips. 'Just no.'

'Why?'

'Because I can't.'

'Or won't?'

'Brian, why is it so important to you?' Sylvie shook her head. 'Everyone knows I'm your girl. Why should it matter whether or not we've been to bed together?'

Brian let her go with a smothered oath. 'If you have to ask that, I'm wasting my time,' he declared harshly. 'Sylvie, don't you ever—*want* to?'

'Not—not specially,' she admitted, wondering with a sudden pang whether there was something wrong with her. Brian was handsome and popular, and all the girls in school had tried to attract his attention, but for more than three months now he had been dating Sylvie. Their association had been good, at least so far as she was concerned, and his early attempts to take their lovemaking beyond the bounds she had set had given way to a steady relationship. But this evening, she realised, he had only been biding his time, and given the impetus of her proposed departure, he was being forced to precipitate his objective.

'I don't get you, do you know that?' he said now, raking back his thick fair hair with an impatient hand. 'You look such a sexy lady, but underneath I guess you don't even know the score, do you?'

Sylvie absorbed this in silence, slightly amazed by his description of herself as a 'sexy lady'. Was that how he saw her? She couldn't believe it. Not after that unfavourable comparison with Margot this afternoon.

'Come on,' he said now, 'I'll take you home. There's not much point in pursuing this, is there? I mean, what with you going away and all. Call me when you get back, and we'll talk it over, hmm? Until then we're free agents, right?'

You mean *you are*, thought Sylvie, but she didn't say anything, and although she had a sinking feeling in her stomach when he left her at her gate, she couldn't wait to examine her reflection once again, to see what she had missed.

Sylvie had never been to Alasyia before, but she knew of it from Margot's descriptions. It was on a peninsula, southeast of Athens, a pine-clad promontory overlooking the blue-green waters of the Aegean. Leon's parents lived in Athens itself, and Sylvie vaguely recalled Aristotle Petronides' leathery-brown face, and his wife's more aristocratic features. They had attended the wedding in London, with evident misgivings, and had insisted on a more orthodox ceremony taking place, once they returned to Athens. Leon's brothers and sisters—he was the second son in a family of eight—had not all been at the wedding, but his elder brother, Andreas, had been best man, and two of his younger sisters had accompanied their parents. Sylvie hardly remembered them, engrossed as she had been in her own role as bridesmaid, and although she supposed she might meet them again, she was not in a hurry to renew their acquaintance. Leon she might be able to handle; Aristotle Petronides was another matter.

Her plane landed in Athens just after four o'clock in the afternoon, and in spite of the warmth of London in early July, nothing had prepared her for the heat wafting up from the tarmac as she stepped out of the aircraft. It was like a blanket, wrapping itself around her and stifling her, and she could well understand why a house at the beach was so desirable. She was glad she had taken her mother's advice and worn a dress, instead of the inevitable trousers she was used to, although the liberal folds of Indian cotton were soon sticking to her legs. Her hair, too, felt hot and heavy, and she entered the airport buildings lifting its silky dampness up from her nape.

It was then that she saw him, a tall man, dressed formally in a grey silk business suit, standing beside a pillar, watching her. He was evidently Greek, although taller and leaner than many of the men around him, and his raven-dark hair was smooth, and not curly, his dark eyes long-lashed and hooded. He was certainly an attractive man, she acknowledged, and yet there was something about that intense scrutiny that troubled her, something vaguely menacing about that frank appraisal. It made her glance about her anxiously, hoping Leon was not far away, bringing an awareness of her own vulnerability, in a country that was unfamiliar to her.

She dragged her gaze away, concentrating on finding her passport in her shoulder bag, checking that she had all the necessary information. Leon had said that he would meet Margot at the airport. She had no reason to feel apprehensive. And it was obvious that a man like the man standing by the pillar would have some objective in coming to the airport in the first place, and not any intention of accosting a girl without any claims to sophistication.

'Excuse me!'

She had been so intent on avoiding the man's eyes, she had failed to notice that the queue she had joined had moved on, and the deep male voice that addressed her sent a ripple of awareness up her spine. Swinging round, she came face to face with her adversary, and her lips parted in dismay when she realised he was blocking her path.

'If you don't mind——' she began, uncaring as to whether or not he understood her, only eager to reach the comparative security afforded by the passport officer, and his somewhat thin lips compressed.

'I think I know you,' he insisted, to her consternation. 'You are—Sylvana Scott, are you not? Margot's sister?' He frowned, as she gazed at him aghast. 'But tell me, what are you doing here? Where is Margot? Is she with you?'

'Wh-who are you?'

Sylvie's lips could scarcely form the words. This wasn't Leon. It certainly wasn't Aristotle Petronides. And yet— and yet there was a resemblance.

'Do you not remember me?' he enquired, although he seemed loath to make the distinction. 'I am Andreas Petronides, Leon's brother. Now will you tell me where Leon's wife is?'

Sylvie licked her lips. Andreas Petronides! Of course— Leon's best man. She would not have recognised him, and yet he had recognised her. Was she so little changed from the child she had been?

'Miss Scott?'

He was speaking again, demanding a reply, and she looked beyond him to where the passport officer was now waiting, the queue having cleared, waiting to clear her passport. Obviously the Petronides name enabled this man to move freely in an area where identification was all important, but that was scarcely important now.

'I—I—shouldn't I pass through passport control first?' she ventured, seizing on the diversion, and his dark eyes narrowed.

'First you will tell me where Margot is,' he insisted, and she caught her lower lip between her teeth so that he should not see her indecision.

'She's not here,' she admitted reluctantly, then gasped

when he caught the softness of her upper arm between his fingers, painfully compressing the flesh.

'What do you mean—she is not here?' he demanded, and then with an eye to the inquisitive stare of the passport officer, he urged her forward. 'Do it,' he said. 'Show him your identification. I will wait for you in the Customs hall.'

Still a little unnerved, Sylvie did as she was told, mildly alarmed by her tacit obedience to his wishes. Was this what Margot had meant when she said Greek men were not like Englishmen? Certainly she could not imagine any man of her acquaintance behaving so arrogantly towards a virtual stranger. It all added to the feeling of alienation that had possessed her, ever since she saw him standing there, as she now knew waiting for her—or waiting for Margot, which was just the same—and she was beginning to realise just how reckless she had been in agreeing to come here.

He was waiting for her beside her suitcases, apparently having arranged that she should be discharged with the minimum amount of fuss. Another man was with him, and her heart sank at the expectation that this might be yet another brother, come to censure her, but his black uniform dispelled her apprehensions. He was evidently a chauffeur, and she hoped with eager urgency that he might be in Leon's employ, and that her interrogation by Andreas Petronides would soon be over.

'Come.'

Clearly that time wasn't quite yet, and Sylvie was obliged to accompany Leon's brother out into the brilliant sunshine that bathed the airport. The chauffeur had taken possession of her cases, and they were stowed into the trunk of a silver-grey limousine waiting for them, and then Andreas stood back politely to allow her to precede him into the capacious back of the car.

Sylvie hesitated. 'Leon——' she began, feeling the need for some reassurance, but Andreas merely gestured more forcibly, and she was obliged to obey him once again.

The limousine was air-conditioned, and after the sticky heat outside Sylvie could not suppress the sigh of relief that escaped her. It was only as the chauffeur seated himself behind the wheel in the partitioned driving compartment, and the car began moving, that she realised she had asked for no identification, and her lips parted anxiously at the awareness of her folly.

But, even as she turned towards the man beside her, he spoke, and what he said temporarily robbed her of any other consideration. 'Now, you will tell me when Margot intends to join us,' he ordered harshly, 'or is she so without conscience that not even the knowledge of her husband's illness is sufficient to bring her home?'

CHAPTER TWO

SYLVIE stared at him for several minutes after he had finished speaking, and then, realising her scrutiny might be misconstrued, she looked down blindly at her hands gripping her bag. Was he serious? Was Leon really ill? And Margot knew about it!

'Now you are going to tell me you did not know, am I right?' he intoned contemptuously, shifting restlessly in his seat. 'Do not bother. I shall not believe you.'

'But it's true!' She looked up then, forced to defend herself, and met the disturbing impact of sceptical dark eyes. 'I didn't know. How—how could I?' She paused. 'Does Margot know?'

'Does Margot know?' he repeated grimly, settling himself lower in his seat and spreading his drawn-up knees, confined by the limitations of the space available. 'Oh, yes, Margot knows. Why else did she send you here?'

'I thought I was coming to look after Nikos for a few weeks,' Sylvie retorted, stung by his insolence and his hostility. 'Margot didn't tell me anything else.' She hesitated. 'But if I'm not needed, why don't you take me straight back to the airport? I believe there's a flight——'

'Wait!' His tone was less aggressive than weary now, and she looked at him apprehensively, prepared for another outburst. 'Do you expect me to believe that you knew nothing about Leon's operation? That Margot told you only that Nikos needed a nursemaid?'

Sylvie shrugged. 'It's the truth, whether you believe it or not.'

He said a word then in his own language, that even

she, with her minuscule knowledge of Greek, knew was
not polite. But, after resting his head against the soft
leather upholstery for a few moments, he levered himself
upright in his seat.

'*Poli kala*,' he said, and it was only when he spoke his
own language that she realised how little accent he possessed in hers, 'I believe you. But that does not solve the
situation.'

To evade her own awareness of his disturbingly intent
gaze, Sylvie hastened into speech. 'Leon,' she said, torturing
the strap of her bag, 'what's wrong with him? I—I can't
believe that Margot thought it was anything serious.'

Andreas's thin mouth turned down at the corners. 'Do
you not? But are not all heart operations serious, *ohi*?'

'Leon has a heart condition?' Sylvie gasped. 'I—I don't
know what to say.'

Andreas studied her troubled features for some minutes,
bringing a wave of hot colour up her neck and over her
face, and then, as if taking pity on her, he looked down at
his hands hanging loosely between his knees. 'Leon had
rheumatic fever when he was a child,' he said, without
expression. 'Recently it was discovered that the valves of
his heart were not functioning properly, so an operation
was advised.'

Sylvie shook her head. 'And—and Nikos?'

Andreas shrugged. 'Nikos is—Nikos. He has been staying
with my mother and father, while Leon was in the hospital.'
He sighed. 'Now that Leon has left the hospital, Margot was
to accompany them home.'

'Oh God!'

Sylvie could not have felt worse. How could Margot
have done this—to her, and to Leon? Didn't she care how
he was? Hadn't she felt the need to go and see him, while
he was in the hospital? It was no wonder that Andreas had
been stunned to find her at the airport. And she dreaded

to think what his parents would say when she turned up in Margot's place.

Turning her head, she stared blindly out of the window. The eight miles between the airport and the city were over, and already they were climbing through the narrow streets that formed the suburbs. Seedy hotels, and uninspiring shops and cafés, gave way to the modern heart of the city, where tree-lined squares were lined with canopied chairs and tables, and marble buildings, breathing an air of antiquity, jostled with tourist stores and travel agencies, and the pseudo-Renaissance palace, used for official functions.

Sylvie started, when Andreas suddenly leaned forward and rapped on the glass partition. The chauffeur slid the partition aside, and they exchanged a few words in their own language. Then, after giving Sylvie a vaguely speculative look, the chauffeur closed the partition again, and braking abruptly, turned off the main thoroughfare into a sun-dappled square. There were trees in the middle of the square, providing a shadowy oasis, where mothers could walk their children; but towering above it was one of the new skyscraper blocks, whose concrete and glass influence could be felt in all the capital cities of the world.

The chauffeur brought the Mercedes to a halt at the foot of the shallow steps leading up to the swinging glass doors of the tall building, but when Sylvie would have moved to get out Andreas's hand, more gently this time, stayed her.

'This is not where my parents live,' he said, slowly and deliberately, and while she was absorbing this he went on heavily: 'I think it would be best if I spoke to my parents—to my brother—first, before they meet you, do you understand? It is a—how do you say it?—fragile situation, *ohi?*'

Sylvie nodded. 'I understand that.' She paused. 'But don't you think it would be better if—if I just went away again——'

'*No!*' He spoke vehemently, expelling his breath as he did so, enveloping her in its wine-sweet odour, creating an intimacy she had never experienced before. How old was this man? she wondered. Thirty-five, thirty-six? Married, no doubt, judging by the rings he wore on his long brown fingers, and yet he aroused her awareness of him as a man, more strongly than Brian, or any of the boys she had known, had done.

'You will stay here,' he advised her now, indicating the building behind her. 'This is my apartment. Oh, do not worry——' this as her eyes widened in surprise, '—my housekeeper, Madame Kuriakis, will take care of you until I return.'

Sylvie looked doubtful. 'Is there any point? I mean—if Nikos doesn't need me——'

'But he does,' essayed Andreas flatly. 'My parents are old, too old to have the care of a six-year-old. And if Margot does not intend to fulfil her responsibilities, it may be that you will be required to fill them for her.'

The chauffeur, who had been waiting patiently outside, responded to Andreas's curt nod and swung open the door. He helped Sylvie out on to the pavement, then stood aside to allow his employer to alight, his dark eyes veiled and enigmatic. Sylvie wondered what he was thinking. If he understood no English, did he know who she was, and what she was doing here? And what interpretation might be put upon this visit to Andreas's apartment?

Apparently her luggage was to remain in the car, for Andreas indicated that she should accompany him, and they mounted the shallow steps and passed through the glass doors into the building. A row of lifts confronted them, and they entered the first that answered Andreas's summons, confined in the small cubicle as it accelerated swiftly upward.

Sylvie was intensely conscious of his nearness in the lift, of the hard muscularity of his body, encased in the dark grey business suit, of the strength he had exhibited so painfully at the airport. He was not like Leon. Her memories of her brother-in-law were of a smaller man, a gentler man, and certainly a much less dangerous man. It was amazing how one's opinions could change, she thought inconsequently. At eleven years of age, Andreas had been only another dark stranger at her sister's wedding. Seven years later he was a man, and she was a woman—although she guessed he might dispute the designation.

It was deliciously cool when they stepped out into the corridor and found themselves confronting white-panelled doors, with the Petronides name spelt out in letters of gold. Andreas brought a handful of keys out of his pocket and inserted one in the lock, then urged Sylvie forward into the apartment.

Her first impression was of light and space, but almost immediately following on these thoughts was her breathless reaction to the view. She could see the Acropolis, the milky-white columns of the Parthenon towering over the city, and viewed over the rooftops of Athens, it had an almost fairytale beauty. She was drawn to the long windows, as if by a magnet, and for several seconds she was unaware that Andreas had left her to find the housekeeper.

When she eventually dragged her eyes away and looked about her immediate surroundings, she felt an uneasy sense of disorientation. Her experiences so far had not prepared her for the luxurious appointments of the apartment, and she drew her skirts aside from bronze miniatures on narrow plinths, and furnishings with the unmistakable veneer of age and antiquity.

It was a spacious room she was in, the floor softly tiled

in russet and gold mosaic, and strewn with Bokhara rugs. A copper-shaded lamp was suspended over velvet-soft hide sofas, dotted with jewel-bright cushions, and a custom-built unit housed books and television set, stereo, and radio equipment. Strangely enough, the accoutrements to contemporary living blended well with their older-day counterparts, and the atmosphere was one of comfortable prosperity—and understated opulence.

The door behind her opened, and she turned to find Andreas re-entering the room, accompanied by a woman, plump, and black-clad, who regarded Sylvie with some suspicion.

'This is Madame Kuriakis,' Andreas introduced them briefly, his dark eyes lingering longer than necessary, Sylvie thought, on hers. '*Apo dho i* Thespinis Scott, *kiria.*'

'*Hero poli, thespinis,*' Madame Kuriakis murmured politely, and then turning to her employer, she evidently asked him some question concerning Sylvie's presence there.

'*Mia stighmi,*' Andreas responded, with a quelling gesture, before continuing in English: 'My housekeeper wishes to know whether you would like something to eat or drink. And then, I am afraid, I must leave you. I shall endeavour not to be too long.'

Sylvie shook her head. 'Perhaps some coffee,' she ventured, unwilling to admit that she felt too churned up inside to eat anything. Then: 'Are you sure I should stay here? Your wife——'

'I have no wife, Miss Scott,' he advised her, with a wry look. '*Fere ligho kafe, kiria,*' this to Madame Kuriakis. '*Herete, thespinis. Sto espanidhin!*'

He left her with a faint smile, and after indicating that Sylvie should take a seat, Madame Kuriakis left her also. It was slightly unnerving being left in such magnificent isolation, and Sylvie felt a growing awareness of her own incongruity in being here. Margot had done this, she thought angrily. Margot had sent her here, to be insulted and humiliated, and the temptation to get to her feet again and escape from this luxurious confinement was almost more than she could bear.

The return of Madame Kuriakis, with a tray on which reposed a silver coffee pot and cream jug, a silver sugar bowl, and a dish of sticky sweetmeats, steadied her. The Greek woman put the tray down on the low table in front of Sylvie's sandal-clad feet, and then knelt to pour the thick black beverage.

'*Krema, thespinis?*' she suggested, pointing to the jug, '*zahari?*'

'No, no, nothing, thank you,' answered Sylvie, waving her hand in negation, and with a little bob of her head the woman rose to her feet again and left the room.

The coffee was treacly-rich, and very strong, and after tasting it Sylvie was glad to resort to the cream and sugar. She added several spoonfuls of sugar to hide the bitter taste, and still grimaced behind her hand after swallowing a mouthful. Still, it was something to do, and she toyed with the tiny silver spoon, and admired the fragile china cup and saucer.

The sweetmeats were more to her liking, although their cloying texture stuck to her teeth. They were probably extremely fattening, too, she reflected, although Andreas didn't appear to have suffered by it.

Thinking of Andreas brought her up from her seat again, and across to the windows. She didn't know why, but she was curiously loath to allow him to occupy her thoughts, and she could only assume it was his attitude towards her which aroused such strong feelings. Margot had been right about one thing, Greek men were not like Englishmen, and she was not altogether sure she liked the distinction.

She wondered now what Leon's letter to Margot had

really said. She doubted her mother knew that Leon had
been in hospital. Mrs Scott might be partisan in some
things, but if she had suspected Leon was ill, surely she
would have urged her daughter to return to Greece.

As for herself, Sylvie was still too disturbed to know
how she felt. Caring for Nikos while his father was going
about his normal business pursuits was one thing; becoming nurse, as well as nursemaid, for his father, too, was
quite another. Besides, Leon would not want her there. It
was Margot he wanted, Margot he had expected, Margot
who should be here.

The time passed slowly, or perhaps it was that Sylvie
was too conscious of the minutes, the hands on the ormolu
clock crawling painfully towards six o'clock. At fifteen
minutes past, the silver-grey telephone rang, and while
Sylvie froze in anticipation Madame Kuriakis came to
answer it.

She expected it to be Andreas, summoning her to the
phone, explaining without the embarrassment of another
confrontation, that Leon and his parents refused to see
her. But Madame Kuriakis scarcely looked at her, speaking into the receiver with evident animation, reassuring,
if it was possible to identify her tone, whoever was on the
line that Andreas's absence was regrettable.

When she replaced the receiver again, she glanced at
Sylvie with reluctant courtesy. 'Thespinis Eleni,' she said,
as if that should mean something, and Sylvie forced a
smile even though she had no idea who Thespinis Eleni
might be.

Left to herself again, she speculated about the caller.
Eleni! That was a woman's name, of course. But what
woman? Not his wife; he had said he had no wife. His
sister, perhaps. Or a cousin. Or more likely, a girl-friend,
she reflected resignedly, realising that whatever else
Andreas Petronides might be, he was not without attrac-

tion for the opposite sex.

The sound of a key in the lock brought her round with a start, to gaze apprehensively across the room. In the fading light there were shadows casting pools of darkness over the mellow floor, but the lean muscular figure of her host was unmistakable.

He came into the room economically, moving with the lithe easy grace she had noticed earlier. He closed the door, dropped his keys into his pocket, and then surveyed her position by the windows with wry contemplation.

'I am sorry I have been so long,' he said at once, unbuttoning his jacket to reveal the tailored lines of his waistcoat. 'But there was much to discuss, as you may imagine. Arrangements to be made.'

'Arrangements?' echoed Sylvie faintly, touching the slender chain about her throat, which was all the jewellery she wore. 'You—you mean, I'm to stay here? In Greece, I mean. But what did your brother say?'

Before he could reply, however, Madame Kuriakis appeared, eager to give him the message she had taken. Sylvie heard the woman's name, Eleni, mentioned several times in their conversation, but apart from that she understood none of it, and stood there in silence, feeling unutterably *de trop*.

Eventually, however, Andreas silenced the housekeeper, and after he had given her some instruction, she disappeared again, leaving Sylvie to face whatever was to come.

'So.' Andreas expelled his breath noisily. 'Now we can continue. And yes, you are to remain in Greece.'

Sylvie found her legs were strangely shaky and moving away from the windows, she sought the refuge of one of the sofas. Somehow she had convinced herself she would be returning to London, and now that she wasn't, she felt curiously weak.

'Your—your brother,' she began, aware of his eyes upon her, and needing to say something to divert him, 'what did he say?'

Andreas shrugged, and then, much to her dismay, he lowered his weight on to the sofa beside her, and giving her a disturbingly gentle look, he said: 'Leon wants to see you. I have explained that you are not to blame for Margot's behaviour,' his lips tightened, 'and he has agreed that you should stay and look after Nikos. As you had intended.'

Sylvie looked bewildered. 'But how? I mean—am I to go to Alasyia with Leon?'

Andreas's jaw hardened. 'Unfortunately, that would not be at all acceptable.'

'Acceptable?' Sylvie was confused.

'You are a young unmarried girl,' declared Andreas roughly. 'Sick as Leon is, he is still a man.'

'Oh!' Her colour deepened. 'So—so what——'

'Arrangements have been made,' said Andreas flatly, and somehow Sylvie knew who had been responsible for those arrangements. 'Leon has been very ill. He needs time to convalesce. It has been arranged that he will continue his convalescence at Monastiros.'

'Monastiros?' Sylvie gazed at him uncomprehendingly. 'Where—where is that?'

Andreas leaned back against the cushioned leather, unfastening the button beneath his silver-grey tie, loosening the knot almost imperceptibly. He looked more relaxed, even satisfied, but Sylvie was impatient to know exactly what he had planned for her.

'Monastiros is an island, *thespinis*,' he said, his eyes narrowed as he looked at her. 'It belongs to—my family. You and Nikos will be happy there, and Leon will have all the care he needs. My aunt, Ariadne Petronides, will see to that.'

Sylvie sat up. 'But why couldn't we go to Alasyia? If—if your aunt is to provide a chaperon?'

'You will go to Monastiros,' he stated flatly. 'It is all decided.' He ran the palm of one hand over the roughening skin of his jawline. 'And now you must excuse me while I change my clothes. My parents wish for us to dine with them this evening.'

Sylvie scrambled to her feet as he stood up, and her haste brought her less than a hand's-breadth away from him. 'I—I can't go to dinner like this,' she stammered, indicating the creased Indian cotton, and without hesitation his dark eyes dropped appraisingly down the full length of her body.

She had never been so conscious of her own shortcomings, she thought, with the blood rising hotly to the surface of her skin. He could not help but observe the palpitating rise and fall of her full breasts, or miss the anxious quivering of her stomach. Beneath the enveloping folds of her dress her knees were shaking, and she was sure she looked as hot and dishevelled as she felt. Nevertheless, his intent assimilation of her appearance did arouse a certain indignation inside her, and she clung to this as his eyes returned to her face.

'Your suitcases are downstairs,' he said at last, without emphasis, moving his shoulders in an indifferent gesture. 'I will have Spiro fetch them up for you.'

The crisp detachment of his tone made Sylvie increasingly aware of her own lack of sophistication. She was over-sensitive, she told herself impatiently. She had no reason to object to his assessment. After all, they were virtually related, he as Leon's brother and she as Margot's sister, but nevertheless no man had looked at her in quite that way, and she was left feeling raw, and strangely vulnerable.

'Th-thank you,' she said now, linking her clammy fingers together, and as he moved away to summon the chauffeur she endeavoured to compose herself. But she couldn't dismiss the trickling of moisture that had invaded her spine, or dispel her awareness of his alien personality.

Madame Kuriakis reappeared, and at Andreas's instigation showed Sylvie into the bedroom she could use to change in. If the housekeeper had any misgivings about the girl's continued presence in the apartment, she managed to conceal them, but Sylvie, with her increased sensitivity, suspected she had very definite opinions of her own.

Left alone, Sylvie explored her domain with genuine curiosity. So this was what Margot had been loath to abandon, she reflected with unusual cynicism, trailing her fingers over apple-green damask and the gleaming patina of polished wood. Even the adjoining bathroom had a sunken bath, with its own *jacuzzi* unit, and she acknowledged without envy that luxury here was an accepted part of living. She was almost regretful she had only time to take a shower, although perhaps it was just as well. It would not do to get too accustomed to so much comfort.

By the time she emerged from the bathroom, a fluffy green towel draped sarong-wise about her, her suitcases had been deposited on the carved chest at the end of the bed. Extracting her keys from her handbag, she opened the largest of them with a thoughtful air and studied its contents with evident indecision.

Expecting to stay at Alasyia, which was sufficiently remote from civilisation to need little in the way of formal clothes, she had brought mostly casual wear and swimsuits. But she could hardly turn up at the Petronides residence for dinner wearing a cotton smock or beachwear, and the nearest thing to an evening outfit she possessed was a waist-coat and matching pants in amber-coloured velvet. It was worn with a cream shirt with wide, flowing sleeves gathered into a lacy cuff, and a frilled jabot below her small determined chin, and Sylvie had always thought it was quite flattering. The amber colour matched her eyes, which were several shades lighter than the rich brown they should have been, and the close-fitting pants accentuated the slender length of her legs. Nevertheless, she suspected that Madame Petronides might not approve, and she viewed the rounded curve of her hips with some anxiety. Was Margot right? Did she wear her clothes too tight? Did she eat all the wrong things? She sighed half irritably. Well, it was Margot's fault that she was here, and if she didn't suit, Margot would have to give up her selfish pursuits and replace her.

She studied the fall of corn-gold hair without satisfaction. Should she braid it, or coil it into a chignon, or leave it loose? Plaiting her hair would only accentuate her immaturity, she decided impatiently, and she didn't really have the time to do a good job of creating a more sophisticated style. With a resigned shrug she tied it at her nape with a length of black cord, then regarded her appearance with as much objectivity as she could muster.

Where was she expected to sleep tonight? she wondered, after dimissing her appearance with a careless shrug. Acting on impulse, she folded up the Indian cotton and re-locked her suitcases, guessing there was little chance that she would be allowed to stay here. The idea that she might be expected to stay with Margot's mother and father-in-law had little appeal for her, but she doubted she would be offered any alternative. If it was unacceptable that she should stay at Alasyia with Leon, it was certainly unacceptable for her to sleep at Andreas's apartment.

When she entered the living room again, Andreas was already waiting for her, his dark looks enhanced by a black mohair dinner jacket. He was in the process of pouring himself a drink from the selection available on a tray resting on a carved wooden table, but he straightened at her entrance and inclined his head politely.

'Can I offer you something?' he enquired, indicating the glass in his hand, but Sylvie shook her head. She was nervous enough as it was, without the effects of alcohol to weaken her confidence, and Andreas shrugged his acceptance and raised his glass to his lips.

Unwilling to appear to be studying him too closely, Sylvie allowed her eyes to move round the lamplit room. It was quite dark outside the long windows now, and the lights of Athens beckoned insistently. Instinctively she moved towards the windows, catching her breath as the floodlit Parthenon attracted her enchanted eyes. She thought she had never seen anything more magnificent than the tall white columns outlined against the velvety darkness of the sky, and her lips parted in unknowing provocation as she gazed upon its ancient symmetry.

'You find it interesting?'

She had been unaware that Andreas had come to stand beside her until he spoke, and now she looked up at him with some of the fascination she had felt still in her eyes.

'It's quite beautiful, isn't it?' she exclaimed, her voice husky with sudden emotion, and Andreas's dark eyes were enigmatic as he met that ingenuous appeal.

'How old are you, Sylvana?' he asked, using her name for the first time, and warm colour surged into her cheeks.

'I'm eighteen,' she replied, answering automatically, but quickly too, as she turned her head away from his cool scrutiny. 'And please call me Sylvie. Everyone does.'

Andreas shrugged. He had disposed of his glass, she noticed, and although she expected him to suggest that it was time they were leaving, he seemed curiously reluctant to abandon his position. Instead, he remained where he was, looking down at her, and it was she who shifted uneasily again, aware of her own lack of sophistication.

'You do not mind—spending these weeks in Greece?' he asked, with narrow-eyed interrogation, and Sylvie shook her head.

'No. No, I don't mind,' she conceded. 'At least—well,' she qualified her statement, 'it was the only thing I could do.'

'You are not like Margot, I think,' he opined dryly. 'At eighteen, I could not imagine her giving up her time to look after her small nephew.'

'Oh——' Sylvie managed a half smile of deprecation, 'I'm not so noble. Who wouldn't enjoy spending a few weeks in this climate!' She made a gesture of dismissal. 'Actually, I'm the lazy one of the family. Ask Mummy or—or Margot, they would tell you. I like lazing around—sunbathing, swimming, reading . . .'

'You are still at school, yes?' he suggested, and now her curiously tawny eyes flashed in annoyance.

'I'm still at school, *no*!' she retorted, unconsciously mocking his cultivated English. 'I left school—some weeks ago. I'm going to university in October.'

Andreas's lean mouth twisted. 'My apologies, *thespinis*,' he offered mockingly. 'It was not my intention to insult you. Forgive me.'

Sylvie sighed. 'You didn't insult me. It's just—well, I'm not a child, you know.'

Andreas inclined his head and now he did begin to move towards the door. 'We must be leaving,' he remarked, flicking back his cuff to consult the plain gold watch on his wrist. 'We have a call to make on our way to my father's house, and I do not wish to be late.'

Sylvie felt suitably chastened, although whether that was his intention, she had no way of knowing. With a feeling of irritation out of all proportion to the incident, she followed him across the room, then halted uncertainly when she remembered her suitcases.

'I—oughtn't we to take my luggage?' she suggested, colouring anew when he turned to give her a preoccupied look. 'I mean—I won't be coming back here, will I?' She hesitated. 'Or will I?'

'It is already arranged that you will stay here tonight,' Andreas remarked, with faintly brusque resolution. 'My sister Marina will return with us this evening, and she also will sleep at the apartment, so long as you are here.'

'So long as I am here?' Sylvie echoed, as she preceded him into the corridor outside, and Andreas closed the door behind them with definite precision.

'It may take several days to reorganise my brother's plans,' Andreas told her, as the lift doors slid smoothly open. 'Surely the prospect of staying in Athens for two or three days more does not distress you?'

'N-o.' But Sylvie was slightly disturbed by the prospect, and by the knowledge that she would be seeing a lot more of Andreas Petronides.

CHAPTER THREE

SPIRO was waiting with the chauffeur-driven limousine, and Sylvie climbed into the back with some reluctance. The night air outside was magical, soft and warm and silky smooth, faintly scented with the perfume from the flowers that grew in such profusion in the gardens surrounding the apartment building.

Andreas gave the chauffeur his instructions, then got in beside her, his weight automatically depressing the cushioned upholstery. Sylvie was intensely conscious of him only inches away from her on the leather seat, his thigh and the powerful length of his leg reclining indólently. Yet he made no attempt to speak to her again, and aware of her impulsive rejoinder earlier, she endeavoured to restore their previous amicability.

'Will—will I be meeting any of the other members of your family this evening—Andreas?' she enquired, using his name deliberately. 'Apart from your mother and father, of course,' she added, and looked at his shadowy profile half defiantly, defending her use of his Christian name. After all, they were distantly related, she told herself again, and she had no intention of compounding his opinion of her youthfulness by addressing him as Mr, or *Kirie*, Petronides.

There was a pregnant silence, when she thought he wasn't going to answer her, but then he said quietly: 'My two youngest sisters are unmarried, and still live with my parents. They will be present this evening, naturally, and Leon will be there, but of course, you know that.'

Sylvie didn't, but she acknowledged that it was reasonable. She wondered if she would see Nikos, too, but perhaps he would already be in bed. She doubted he would recognise her. Apart from one visit to London with both his parents when he was three years old, her only contact with her nephew had been through the medium of Christmas and birthday cards, and the occasional family photograph.

She was considering this when the limousine began to slow down, and she saw through the windows of the car that they had entered a quiet square, lined with tall white-painted houses. It was evidently a residential square, many of the houses possessing shutters and colourful window boxes, and the limousine halted at the foot of a flight of steps leading up to a narrow black door.

'A moment,' said Andreas, by way of explanation, and without waiting for the chauffeur he thrust open his door and stepped out on to the pavement. As he did so, the door to the house opened and a young woman appeared, bidding goodbye to whoever was behind the door, and descending the steps eagerly towards them. She was tall and slim and elegant, her full-skirted dress swinging gracefully about her knees, her dark hair shoulder-length, and tipped slightly upward. She was very attractive, in a dark Grecian sort of way, and Sylvie watched with some envy as Andreas bent to kiss her, and her hand strayed possessively over the fine mohair of his collar. She knew without being told that this had to be Eleni, and she guessed her call earlier had been returned, and the new arrangements explained to her.

Andreas led the girl back to the car, and she climbed inside as gracefully as she had descended the steps, seating herself beside Sylvie and bestowing upon her a rather tentative smile. How old was she? Sylvie wondered. Twenty-one or twenty-two? She couldn't be much older, but her manner was shy and reserved. Sylvie, for her part, smiled in return, and encountered Andreas's thoughtful appraisal as he got back into the vehicle.

'Eleni, I'd like you to meet Leon's sister-in-law, Sylvana,' he remarked, seating himself on one of the pull-down seats in front of them, as the limousine moved off again. 'She is going to look after Nikos, until his mother feels capable of meeting her responsibilities.'

'Oh, but——' Sylvie opened her mouth to protest that that was not at all the arrangement, but Eleni forestalled her. 'How do you do, Sylvana,' she greeted her politely, holding out a slim white hand for Sylvie to take. 'Andreas has told me of your kindness in coming here. I hope you will enjoy your stay in our country.'

'I'm sure I shall.' Sylvie shook hands with Eleni, and forced some enthusiasm into her voice, but she couldn't help wishing her situation was not so ambiguous. *What about Dora?* she wanted to cry, but so far the nursemaid's name had not been mentioned.

Eleni folded her hands in her lap, and Sylvie noticed the exquisitely designed ruby, set in a circlet of diamonds, that occupied the third finger of her left hand. An engagement ring? she pondered. Andreas's, perhaps? So far he had said nothing about the girl but her name.

Her presence prevented Sylvie from asking any more questions. She could hardly question Andreas about his relationship to the girl, with Eleni sitting there listening, and besides, he seemed quite content to exchange an occasional word with the Greek girl, in their own language, of course.

Presently, however, Eleni turned to her again. 'How is Margot, Sylvana?' she asked, surprising her by the question. Then she added: 'We met last year, at Michael's wedding. Do you know Michael, Sylvana? He is Andreas's youngest brother.'

'I'm afraid not.' Sylvie shook her head. 'And do call me Sylvie. Sylvana's such a mouthful!'

'Such a what? A mouthful?' Eleni looked confused, and Andreas broke in to explain.

'She means—it is too long, too formal, Eleni,' he said, glancing coolly at the younger girl. 'She wishes you to address her as Sylvie.'

'Oh, I see.' Eleni gave a rueful little laugh, and Sylvie felt bound to elucidate.

'My mother chose rather—flowery names,' she confessed apologetically. 'And while Margot is—well, Margot, I've always thought of myself as Sylvie.'

Eleni gave a small shrug of her shoulders. 'Oh, I see. *Poli kala.* So—is your sister ill? Is that why she has sent you to act as her deputy?'

Sylvie was conscious of Andreas looking at her too now, and guessed her reply was of interest to him as well. So far, he had not questioned her as to Margot's activities, and Sylvie had hoped to make her explanations to Leon himself. But for all Eleni's demure attitude, she had her full quota of curiosity, and although her question sounded innocent enough, it was disturbingly pointed.

'Margot is—not ill,' Sylvie answered now, looking somewhat defiantly at the man opposite. 'Surely you know—surely Leon has told you—Margot is an actress, or rather she was before she was married.'

'I understood Margot's acting career was sunk some months before she and Leon were married,' Andreas inserted now, his tone cold and precise, and Sylvie felt her cheeks begin to burn again.

'Well, it might have—floundered a little,' she agreed, in some confusion, 'but it wasn't—sunk. And—and when her agent learned she was living in London again——'

'Do you not mean—*staying* in London?' asked Andreas harshly, and Sylvie felt hopelessly out of her depth.

'All right,' she said. 'Staying in London, then. Anyway, he—he offered her a part, a good part, the kind of part she has always wanted.'

'You mean he made her an offer she could not refuse?' suggested Andreas contemptuously, and Sylvie sighed.

'I suppose so.'

'Why did you not tell me this sooner?'

'I—I was going to. But—but then, when you told me Leon had been ill——'

'—you were ashamed!'

'I was—*shocked*!' she amended indignantly. 'I was,' she added, meeting his cynical gaze, visible even in the subdued lighting from the street outside. 'Honestly, Mummy and I had no idea Leon had been ill.'

'I said I believed you,' Andreas retorted, drawing a heavy breath. 'But it occurs to me that perhaps you ought not to tell Leon so.'

Sylvie swallowed convulsively. 'Not tell him?'

'That is correct.' Andreas contemplated the traffic beyond the windows with narrow-eyed concentration. 'He has suffered enough shocks for one day. Your arrival instead of Margot was an immense disappointment to him, as you can imagine. To further add that you were unaware of his condition—that Margot had chosen not to tell you—had regarded it so lightly——' He broke off with a grim tightening of his mouth. 'I suggest you refrain from admitting so damning an indictment.'

Sylvie bent her head. 'Yes, I see.'

'Later on, perhaps——' Andreas moved his shoulders indifferently, 'we shall see.'

'Poor Leon!' Sylvie, who had almost forgotten Eleni's presence, started as the Greek girl offered her condolences. 'He should never have marr——'

She broke off at this point, but not before Sylvie had interpreted what she had intended to say, and although she gazed at Andreas in some consternation, Sylvie had no doubts that Eleni had intended her to understand.

'I agree,' she said now distinctly, regarding the Greek
girl with a cool arrogance she was far from feeling. 'But
they are married, aren't they? And there's nothing any of
us can do about it. And besides, there is Nikos to consider.'

Eleni looked somewhat taken aback by the younger
girl's candour, and Sylvie was pleased. It was only as she
looked at Andreas, and met his cold appraisal, that she
realised how unforgivably she had abused the Greek girl's
discretion.

The Petronides' house was in Syntagnia Avenue, one of
the most fashionable areas of the city. Although many of
the old town houses, occupied by the wealthier families of
Athens, had given way to tall modern blocks of flats,
Syntagnia Avenue retained its individuality, and all the
houses here stood in their own grounds. It was set on one
of the northern slopes overlooking the city, and Sylvie's
eyes were wide when they approached tall iron gates that
opened electronically to admit them. Margot had told
her a little about her in-laws—their wealth, and influence,
their power and their possessions; but nothing had
prepared her for this palatial mansion, with its classical
architecture and stately Doric columns.

As she followed Eleni out of the car, she was conscious
of the scent of magnolias, the source of which soon became
evident. Trees of magnolia and bushes of hibiscus brushed
her sleeve as she looked about her, their perfume overlying
the warmth of the night air with a sweetness that was
almost cloying.

Heavy wooden doors had opened upon their arrival,
and now a white-coated manservant was waiting to escort
them indoors. Andreas, however, strode on ahead, and
Sylvie followed slowly, absorbing her surroundings.

Beyond the heavy doors was a wide square hallway,

marble-tiled and cool, brilliant with huge bowls of blossoms from the garden. The walls were plain, but adorned with softly-woven tapestries, in a multitude of colours, their jewel-bright radiance competing with the more conservative patina of polished silver and brass. A darkly carved staircase gave access to an upper story, lit by lamps of beaten bronze, and there were other lamps in the window embrasures, highlighting the jewelled icons with their sombre iron crosses.

Andreas had disappeared, and Eleni with him, but as Sylvie looked about her with some apprehension she saw a young girl watching her from an open doorway. She was small and plump, with curly black hair and dancing eyes, that sparkled in anticipation when she saw their guest.

'Sylvana!' she exclaimed, coming forward, and now Sylvie could see they were much of an age. 'It is Sylvana, is it not?' she repeated, smiling encouragingly. 'You do not remember me, do you? I am Marina. Remember? I came to England when your sister married my brother.'

'Marina! Of course.' In truth, Sylvie could only vaguely remember the two little Greek girls who had accompanied their parents to London. But it was good to know that Marina remembered, and she smiled at Andreas's sister with genuine sincerity.

But before they could continue their conversation, a group of people emerged through an archway that evidently led to another part of the house. Behind them, Sylvie could see Andreas and Eleni, but confronting her were her sister's mother and father-in-law, and Leon himself, in a wheelchair.

Immediately she felt defensive, even with Marina standing beside her. Leon's mother and father looked anything but welcoming, and even Leon himself seemed lost for words.

'Hello,' she said, taking the matter into her own hands and crossing to her brother-in-law's chair. Taking the hand he offered, she shook it gently, then bent deliberately and kissed his cheek. 'How are you, Leon?' she asked him warmly. 'I'm so sorry you've been unwell.'

Leon's pale face cracked, and he offered her a slight smile. Sylvie suspected he didn't smile much these days, and unconsciously her heart went out to him. He looked so thin and frail, emaciated almost, and although she knew he was almost as tall as Andreas, he seemed shrunken sitting in the canvas chair.

'It is good of you to come, Sylvie,' he told her firmly, and she was glad that at least one member of the Petronides family knew of the shortening of her name. That would be due to Margot's influence, she supposed. Margot never addressed her as Sylvana.

'I—I was glad to,' she said now, glancing rather defiantly at Andreas. 'I'm looking forward to meeting Nikos again. Where is he? Is he here? Will I get to see him soon?'

'Soon enough,' declared Leon's father rather harshly, as he and Leon's mother came forward to offer their own greetings. 'So little Sylvana has grown up, eh? You are welcome, child. Nikos will be happy to see you.'

Madame Petronides looked less enthusiastic. 'I trust you had a good journey, Sylvana,' she said, in heavily accented English, her dark eyes appraising Sylvie's pants suit without approval. She, like Eleni and Marina, was wearing a dress, its simple lines belying its undoubted exclusiveness. 'Your mother is well, I hope. We seldom correspond these days.'

Sylvie smiled, and assured her hostess that her mother was fine, all the while aware that what they really wanted to ask was: *Where was Margot?* and *Why hadn't she come?*

But discretion prevailed, and Madame Petronides, who

had wheeled her son's chair into the hall, now took charge
of it again to lead the way along a wide carpeted corridor.
Marina accompanied them, walking with Sylvie, while
Andreas and Eleni walked with his father, and Sylvie was
glad of the girl's company in this faintly inimical gathering.

'Nikos is in bed,' Marina confided in a low tone. 'It is
not good to excite him late at night, you understand? He
is—how do you say it?—strung up?'

'Highly strung?' suggested Sylvie doubtfully, realising
that like Andreas and Leon, and all the other members of
his family, Nikos was expecting to see his mother, and
Marina nodded.

'That is so—highly strung,' she agreed vigorously.
'Since Margot went away he has many bad dreams, no?'

'You gossip too much, Marina,' her mother admonis-
hed, overhearing their conversation and glancing round
reprovingly. 'Nikos is like any other small boy. He has the
imagination.' She paused. 'But, naturally, we did not wish
to upset him tonight.'

Marina grimaced when her mother turned away, and
moved her shoulders expressively. 'Mama wanted to tell
Nikos that his mother was not coming,' she whispered to
Sylvie behind her hand, 'but Andreas would not let
her.'

Sylvie's response to this not unexpected confidence was
muted by their entrance into a large, imposing apartment.
Sylvie supposed it was a salon, or a drawing room, or
perhaps simply a reception room, but whatever its designation, it was certainly impressive. It was not a clut-
tered room, indeed its lines were excessively plain, but it
was this as much as anything that added to its formality.
From a high, moulded ceiling, the textured walls were
inset with long sculpted windows, hung with heavy silk
drapes in shades of blue and turquoise. The gilt-edged

mirrors, set at intervals about the walls, reflected stiffly formal chairs, and tables of marble, the patina of polished wood only broken by a bowl of long-stemmed lilies. Their delicate perfume fitted the room, creating an almost sepulchral atmosphere, but although it was undoubtedly spectacular, Sylvie did not like it. She was almost prepared to believe she had been brought here deliberately, for some sort of family inquisition, but none of the others appeared awed by their surroundings, and she guessed familiarity bred contempt.

An aproned maid waited to offer them drinks before dinner, and copying Marina's example, Sylvie took a tall glass of some light pale-coloured liquid. She was not accustomed to alcohol, but this seemed innocent enough, and it was not until Marina had sipped hers and breathed: 'Champagne! Is it not delicious?' that she realised that was what it was.

While his mother was involved in conversation with Eleni, Leon took the opportunity to propel himself across the room towards Sylvie. He exchanged a look with Marina, who had been keeping her company, and then, when she made her excuses and joined her father and Andreas, Leon suggested that Sylvie should sit down on the chair beside him.

'You know why I wish to speak with you, I am sure,' he remarked in a low tone, after she was seated. 'Andreas had no information earlier as to why Margot is not here. I want you to tell me the truth. Does she want a divorce?'

'*No!*' Sylvie's denial was uttered on a rising note, which she quickly stifled as other eyes turned questioningly in their direction. 'No,' she repeated, half inaudibly. 'Honestly, Leon, that's the truth.'

'Then why is she not here?' he demanded, his dark eyes glittering with suppressed emotion. 'She knows the situation. She knows I am unable to come to London at this time.'

Sylvie expelled her breath unevenly. 'Leon, she's got a part—in a play. You know the kind of thing she does. Well——' she sighed, 'it's a good part for her, and she wants to do it. It—it means a lot to her.'

'More than we do,' remarked Leon bitterly, his thin hands moulding the arms of his wheelchair.

Sylvie hesitated. 'I—I don't think that's true,' she ventured, albeit unconvincingly. 'She—she just—needs this—stimulation. But she needs you, too. In her own way.'

Leon's mouth tightened. 'You mean as a safety net, do you not? In case this career she is pursuing does not work out.'

Sylvie shook her head. 'No.' Though she had said virtually the same thing ten days ago. 'Leon, give her a break. Let her try and prove herself. She may fail.'

Leon looked down at his knees, swathed by a soft fur rug. 'I have given her many breaks, Sylvie,' he said heavily. 'How many does she expect?'

Sylvie felt terrible. If only she had known Leon was ill, she would never have agreed to come here, not under any circumstances. It was the support of a wife Leon needed at this time, a mother for Nikos. How could Margot be so callous?

'Have you told my brother why Margot is not here?' enquired Andreas's harsh tones above their heads, and Sylvie looked up in sudden confusion.

'Yes.' It was Leon who answered, leaning back in his chair now, his hands on the arms relaxing almost submissively. 'She has told me, Andreas. It seems I must be patient once again.'

'Patient!' Andreas's lips twisted. 'I would not be so understanding, I fear.'

'But you are not like me, are you, Andreas?' Leon

countered, with a dry smile. 'As yet, no woman has invaded that cynical heart of yours.' He lifted his hands for a moment, then let them fall. 'Not even Eleni, I suspect.'

Andreas acknowledged his brother's gentle cajolery with a casual shrug of his shoulders, but he made no response to it, even though Sylvie's ears had sharpened at the mention of the Greek girl's name. Instead he turned his attention to her, looking down at her with cool assessing eyes, making her overwhelmingly aware of his earlier antagonism towards her.

'My father suggests that perhaps you might like to come and visit Nikos tomorrow morning,' he said, his tone only a couple of degrees higher than the chilly reproval he had offered her in the car. 'Does that appeal to you, *thespinis*, or would you rather go sightseeing?'

Sylvie moistened her lips. 'I'll come here, of course,' she declared, maintaining her composure with an effort. 'I didn't come to Greece to go sightseeing, as you very well know.'

'Good.' Andreas was dismissive. 'I will tell my father of your decision. I myself can bring you, on my way to the office.'

'That's not necessary——' began Sylvie quickly, deciding she could more easily take a taxi, but Leon intervened.

'Sylvie is staying here, is she not?' he exclaimed. 'There is no need for her to go back to your apartment.'

'On the contrary,' retorted Andreas inflexibly. 'It is all decided. She and Marina are to sleep at the apartment, until you leave for Monastiros.'

'But why?' Leon sighed, and Andreas attempted to explain.

'Rooms were prepared for Margot, not for her sister, Leon,' he stated flatly. 'You would not have—Sylvana—

occupying those apartments adjoining yours.'

'There are other apartments,' protested Leon wearily, the effort of arguing evidently exhausting him, and Andreas put a half impatient, half soothing hand on his shoulder.

'It is easier this way, believe me!' he declared gently, and Leon had to accede to his brother's arrangements.

Dinner was announced a few moments later, and this time Sylvie took charge of Leon's chair. 'Please—let me,' she said, when Andreas would have taken it from her, and with a gesture of indifference he went to join his fiancée. For she was his fiancée, Sylvie felt sure of it, and she knew a moment's sympathy for the Greek girl in netting so overbearing and unpredictable a catch.

The dining room was just as impressive as the reception room had been. Long sideboards flanked walls decorated with carved wooden murals, and the enormous table would have seated more than twenty people comfortably. The Petronides' other unmarried daughter, Persephone, joined them for the meal, but after greeting Sylvie with formal politeness, she spent the rest of the evening in conversation with her mother. They were very much alike, whereas Marina resembled her father, and judging by the glances Sylvie occasionally felt in her direction, her presence was a source of some provocation to them.

Sylvie could only suppose they did not approve of Leon's attention to her. Yet her brother-in-law seemed to relax during the course of the meal, and under his gentle encouragement she talked quite freely of her own activities. She told him of her interest in antiquity, and how she had succeeded in her ambition to gain a place at Oxford, and she made him laugh when she bemoaned her efforts to keep slim, and her fateful love of chocolates and fatty foods. She was conscious that Andreas's eyes, too, were often upon them during the meal, but she hoped he would not intervene and spoil their tentative friendship. She had hardly known Leon before this meeting, but after only a couple of hours in his company, she could quite see why Margot had been attracted to him. He was kind, and he was sympathetic; and she felt that she could rely on him, which was reassuring after Andreas's hostility.

When the meal was over, Marina was despatched to collect her overnight things, and Leon's father took the opportunity to have a few words with their young guest.

'Andreas tells me Margot is acting again,' he said, bringing up the subject Sylvie least wanted to discuss, and she forced herself to explain the circumstances.

'Her agent found her this part in a new play,' she said, shifting a little uncomfortably beneath his penetrating stare. Like his eldest son, Aristotle Petronides had the ability to impale her with his eyes, and she found it almost impossible to look away.

'And left you to—how do you say it?—carry the can, no?' he enquired dryly, and a little of her tension eased at the gentleness of his tone. 'Relax, Sylvana—or is it Sylvie? I heard Leon call you that earlier. This is not the den of wolves you think it. We are only human, and Leon is very dear to us.'

'I—I appreciate that.' Sylvie moved her shoulders helplessly. 'I'm sure if Margot had realised——'

'I think Margot realised very well,' replied Leon's father heavily. 'But now we will say no more about it. I am sure Nikos will find the prospect of a new playmate just as appealing as a mother he scarcely knows.'

It was a damning criticism of Margot's role as a mother, but Sylvie could not dispute it. Margot had not been cut out for motherhood, and there was no use pretending to these people, who knew her so well, that her sister had anything more than a desultory interest in the welfare of her son.

Sylvie was sitting with Leon again, when Andreas came to tell her they were leaving.

After dinner, coffee had been served in another of the imposing withdrawing rooms, and earlier, Sylvie had watched Andreas at the grand piano, which occupied one corner of the apartment. He had lounged lazily before the keys, with Eleni draped gracefully beside him, picking out a tune here and there, and just occasionally breaking into some haunting melody that was over far too soon as far as Sylvie was concerned. That he was an accomplished musician she had no doubt, without Leon's casual reference to a talent wasted.

'Andreas could have attended the Conservatoire, in Paris,' he remarked, smiling without envy, as his brother improvised on a theme by Schubert. 'But my father would never have forgiven him, if he had not taken on the mantle for which he was born.' He sighed. 'It is as well he can separate the two halves of his personality. There is no place for sentiment in business.'

Sylvie doubted Andreas was over sentimental. She did not believe one had necessarily to *feel* for the music. Andreas had a talent, which he projected quite expertly, but that was all. His skill did not demand emotion, only complete concentration.

And now Andreas was standing over her again, informing her politely that they would be leaving shortly, making her overwhelmingly aware of his influence over all their actions. He had said he believed her when she told him that Margot had not confided the truth about Leon's illness to her, and yet there was still censure in his dark eyes as they rested upon her. What was it? Did he secretly believe that as sisters she and Margot must be tarred with the same brush? Or was it simply that he objected to her blossoming friendship with Leon, seeing in it the seeds of other disasters? Whatever his inner feelings, his tone was

detached and courteous, and Sylvie wondered if any warm
emotion had ever ruffled that cold façade.

'I will see you tomorrow,' said Leon, as Sylvie rose
from her chair to make her farewells. 'Goodnight, Sylvie.
Sleep well.'

'I shall.' Sylvie bent impulsively and kissed his cheek.
'Until tomorrow, then. I'll look forward to it. And to
meeting Nikos again.'

Andreas took his own leave of his brother, and while
Sylvie bid goodbye to his mother and father, he went to
speak to Eleni. Unwillingly, Sylvie's eyes followed his
progress as he crossed the room, the lithe, easy stretch of
his legs that took him to the Greek girl's side. There was
a curiously tight feeling in her chest as she watched him
stop beside Eleni, inclining his head towards her as she
looked up into his face, and she didn't altogether understand her sudden resentment. It was as if she had abruptly
become aware that even without Margot's damning influence on the situation, to Andreas she was little more
than the child she had been at his brother's wedding. It
was not incomprehensible, she supposed. He was an older,
and much more sophisticated, man. But she wished he
would give her the credit for having some maturity, and
not behave as if she was an annoying encumbrance he
was obliged to take care of.

CHAPTER FOUR

SYLVIE was up early the next morning.

She had slept surprisingly well in the wide comfortable bed, surprisingly, because she had expected the events of the day would prevent her mind from relaxing. But the air, and the food, accomplished what determination could not, and she lost consciousness almost as soon as her head touched the pillow.

She awakened with a tremendous sense of well-being that was quickly dissipated by the remembrance of why she was here. But she determined not to let Margot's lingering carelessness spoil what could be a wonderful holiday, and sliding out of bed she went straight to the windows.

Her room overlooked the back of the apartment building, where the gardens surrounding the tall skyscraper block gave on to a small area of parkland. Even at this early hour there were people about, and she could hear the hum of traffic from the busy heart of the city only a few hundred yards away. There were even joggers in the park, a distinct reminder of the parks back home, and a smile curved her lips as she watched them trot by.

There was no sound that anyone in the apartment was up yet, and after ascertaining that it was barely six-thirty, Sylvie wasn't really surprised. After all, it had been quite late when they returned the night before, and after escorting Sylvie and his sister up to the apartment, Andreas had departed again to take Eleni home. Apparently it had not been to his advantage to make the detour, and take Eleni home in the same way as they had picked her up on the way to his parents' house. Clearly he intended to have a private conversation with her, and as she and Marina had gone straight to bed, Sylvie did not know what time Andreas had returned.

Turning from the windows, and the rose-tinted beauty of the day just beginning, Sylvie paced restlessly about the bedroom. It was already warm, and although she had left the air-conditioning on in her room all night, she felt no sense of chill in her brief cotton nightshirt. Indeed, she could have done without the elbow-length sleeves it sported, and although there was a low vee in front, her hand probing the neckline encountered moist flesh.

She was dying for a cup of tea. The night before, she had drunk only the glass of champagne and one glass of wine with her dinner, the coffee that was served afterwards proving too thick and strong for her taste. In consequence, she was thirsty, and although there was plenty of water in the tap, even the cold was inclined to be tepid. Tea was what she really fancied, a cup of hot sweet tea, and after another tentative examination of her watch she wondered if she dared go and make herself some. She had a fair idea where the kitchen was, and a kitchen was a kitchen, after all. Anyone could boil a kettle, and surely she would find the tea caddy without too much difficulty.

Opening her bedroom door, she stood for a few moments on the threshold, listening. But the apartment was silent, no one stirred, and gaining a little confidence, she padded along the carpeted hall to the living room.

The blinds could not have been closed the night before, and sunlight flooded the floor with its golden rays. It winked on the bronze lamps, and added colour to the hide sofas, and accentuated that sense of space and colour Sylvie had appreciated the previous afternoon. In the morning light, the columns of the Acropolis looked like the backcloth to some ancient Greek drama, the shafts of sunlight reflected from the marble, like spotlights highlighting an empty stage.

Smiling at the fanciful notions of her imagination, Sylvie dragged herself away from the windows, and padded across the soft rugs to the door through which Madame Kuriakis had appeared the day before. She guessed this was the way to the domestic offices of the apartment, and she was proved right. A short hall gave access to swing doors which led into a large, modern kitchen, and she looked about her admiringly before doing anything else.

It was spacious, like the rest of the apartment, with every kind of electrical convenience. A kind of control panel, set into the wall behind the fitted units, regulated a variety of implements, from food-mixers and blenders to the sophisticated mechanism of the refuse disposal. There were the usual machines for washing and drying dishes, and refrigerating food, as well as a split-level cooker with two ovens and a barbecue spit. It was all very space-age and modern, and Sylvie could imagine her mother's delighted reaction if she were faced with such an assortment of gadgets.

Shrugging a little bemusedly, Sylvie padded barefoot across the cork tiles. The electric kettle was filled and ready to be turned on, and feeling slightly daring, she pressed the switch.

While the kettle boiled, she examined the contents of the cupboard above the veined marble worktop. Sure enough, there were jars of coffee beans, just waiting to be ground, and several different kinds of tea, from West Ceylon, to some incomprehensible Chinese variety. Sylvie selected the one that looked least expensive, and was spooning some into a silver-plated teapot when the distinct sound of a door closing came to her ears.

Madame Kuriakis, she guessed, not without some apprehension. She doubted now that the housekeeper would

appreciate one of her employer's guests helping herself to
tea in the kitchen, and what had seemed a rather exciting
adventure became suddenly an invasion of privacy. She
stood there, disconsolately, hopelessly embarrassed at her
obvious state of undress, her bare legs from the thigh down
seeming far more indecent than they had ever done, even
in a bikini. How could she explain that she had been
longing for a cup of tea? The woman didn't even speak
English! Her only hope was an instinctive understanding
of the situation, and she smoothed her unbrushed hair
nervously, preparing her mimed excuses.

The kitchen door swung open without preamble, and
Sylvie's mouth went dry. It was not Madame Kuriakis
who had caught her helping herself to his hospitality, but
Andreas Petronides himself, flushed and unfamiliar, in a
dark green track-suit, with a narrow red band running
down the arm and leg seams.

Sylvie didn't know which of them was the most taken
aback: she, in the skimpy blue and white striped nightshirt, her face almost as red as the bands of his tracksuit,
or Andreas, riveted by the sight of her in his kitchen, when
he had obviously expected to see Madame Kuriakis. He
had even opened his mouth to speak as he came through
the door, but Sylvie's apologetic face made him catch his
words back.

'Sylvana!' he said instead, and she knew her name had
been torn from him. '*Theos*, what are you doing in here?'

Sylvie sighed, moving her shoulders unhappily. 'Oh,
I'm sorry,' she exclaimed. 'I thought no one was up. I
was just making myself a cup of tea. I know it's probably
not the done thing, but I was so thirsty!'

Andreas was still holding the swinging door, but now he
let it go almost abstractedly. 'If you had wanted tea, you
should have rung for Madame Kuriakis,' he said, half
impatiently, his eyes flicking away from her scarcely-clad

figure. 'Are you in the habit of running about the house half naked, for I should tell you, it is not something you should pursue here.'

Sylvie sighed. 'I'm not half naked,' she protested, even though she knew he was right. 'I—I wear much less than this on the beach, and no one's ever objected before.'

Andreas's mouth compressed. 'Where is Madame Kuriakis?'

'I don't know.' Sylvie shrugged again. 'She isn't up yet, I suppose.' She paused, as the kettle began to boil noisily behind her, and she turned to make the tea. 'Will you have some tea with me—Andreas? Or do I have to drink alone?' She forced her tone to remain light, determined not to let him upset her as he had done the day before. 'Or don't you drink tea?'

Andreas hesitated, glancing at his watch. 'Madame Kuriakis will be here in—five minutes. Perhaps I will wait for her.'

Sylvie folded her arms, unaware that by doing so she was shortening the shirt to thigh length only. 'Don't you think I can make tea?' she asked, with mild sarcasm, and then noticed that his hair was damp. 'Oh, is it raining? I thought it was a beautiful morning!'

'It is.' Andreas's tone was curiously harsh, and his eyes when they met hers were not entirely steady. 'I have been to my club. It is a sporting club, only a short way from here. I have been swimming.'

'How nice!' Sylvie meant it. She could think of nothing she would like better at the moment than to swim in a cool pool. 'I thought you'd still be sleeping. As it was so late when you got home last night.'

Andreas did not ask the obvious question, but shrugged and turned away, unzipping the jerkin of his track-suit as he did so, and exposing a brown expanse of chest. The sight of his muscled body, only lightly spread with damp whorls of hair, that funnelled down towards his navel, did strange things to Sylvie. Strange, because although she was used to seeing boys and men of her acquaintance in shorts and swimming gear, she had never before felt such a disturbing sensation in the pit of her stomach. It seemed to uncoil about her abdomen, spreading uncontrollably into her legs, and making her overwhelmingly aware of her own femininity. Her lips parted, to allow more air into her suddenly straining lungs, and an involuntary shiver spread over her skin. What was wrong with her? He wasn't even looking at her. Yet she was aware of him with every nerve in her being.

With deliberate effort she turned back to the teapot, lifting down two teacups and saucers from the cupboard, and saying casually: 'Are you sure you won't have some tea? There's plenty. If—Madame Kuriakis won't object, of course.'

Andreas expelled his breath heavily, and she turned to look at him with raised eyebrows. 'Very well,' he said, and her heart thumped heavily as she met that half aggressive stare. 'Will you bring it into the living room? I need to get my robe.'

'All right,' Sylvie nodded, clattering the cups into their saucers as the draught of his passing set the doors swinging again. Goodness, she thought, rubbing her moist palms together, she had actually persuaded him to change his mind, and in spite of her previous resentment towards him, she felt a trembling sense of anticipation at this unexpected interlude.

By the time she carried the tray into the living room, Andreas had shed the jerkin of his track-suit and replaced it with a wine-coloured terrycloth bathrobe. The robe was belted securely around his waist, and it was only as she handed him his tea that she defined that his purpose had been to suggest a similar course to her. But it was too hot to wear a dressing gown, she thought crossly, picturing herself wrapped in the woolly pink candlewick which was all she possessed, and she resigned herself to his censure as she curled up on a squashy cream sofa.

'Do you usually swim every morning?' she asked, endeavouring to keep the conversation going, as Andreas stood to drink his tea, staring broodingly out of the window.

'Not every morning,' he conceded, after a moment's hesitation, and Sylvie sighed, as the minutes stretched.

'Can't you sit down?' she demanded at last, stung by his detachment. 'I—I'd like to talk about Nikos. And—and about Dora.'

'Dora?' Andreas frowned as he walked back to the sofa, and bent to replace his cup on the tray. 'Oh, yes, Dora. It is a pity she had to leave so suddenly. Nikos was fond of her.'

Sylvie breathed a little more easily. For a moment she had wondered if Margot had lied about Dora, too, but apparently she had been telling the truth.

'I understand her mother has been taken ill,' she added, eager to retain his attention, but now Andreas's frown returned again.

'I did not know that,' he remarked, disturbing Sylvie anew. 'I understood she left because she was getting married. But perhaps her mother's illness was a contributing factor.'

Sylvie pursed her lips. Perhaps, she thought bitterly, or perhaps not. It seemed there was no end to Margot's duplicity. So how many weeks did she expect her sister to stay in Greece? *Indefinitely!*

'Is something wrong?' To her consternation, Andreas had now taken her advice and seated himself on the chair immediately opposite. He sat with his legs apart, his hands hanging loosely between, and his intent dark face was infinitely disturbing in her agitated state.

'It's nothing,' she muttered now, loath to provoke any further hostility between them. 'I—tell me about Nikos. Is he like Leon? It's so long since I saw him.'

'You should have visited,' remarked Andreas quietly, and Sylvie's smile was unknowingly wistful as she acknowledged his statement. 'Were you invited?' he probed, and faint colour invaded her cheeks.

'Does it matter?' She moved her shoulders defensively, running the fingers of one hand up and down the curve of her leg between the ankle and the knee. 'I'm here now, and I'm really looking forward to spending some time with my nephew.'

'Yes.' Andreas studied her averted profile thoughtfully. 'Well, I am sure Nikos will be pleased to see you. He is a friendly boy, a little over-sensitive at times, but lovable for all that.' He paused. 'We must see that you enjoy yourself, too. After all, you have given up your holiday.'

Sylvie, meeting his unexpectedly sympathetic gaze, knew a moment's impatience. 'You don't have to feel sorry for me, you know,' she declared, tossing her head, and he suddenly smiled.

'I do not,' he said, and as he looked at her, her own lips parted in acceptance of her own defiance.

'What do you do?' she asked, wanting to know him. 'Do you work in Athens? Do you live here all the time?'

Andreas looked down at his hands. 'I work in Athens, yes,' he agreed evenly. 'I work for my father. But I travel, too, mostly to Japan, or the United States.'

'It sounds exciting.' Sylvie meant it. 'I'd like to travel. So far I've only been to Austria—oh, and here, of course.'

'Austria?' Andreas looked questioningly at her.

'For the skiing,' Sylvie explained. 'With the school.' She grimaced. 'Last year I sprained my ankle.'

Andreas's eyes grew a little guarded. 'I am sorry.'

'Don't be.' Sylvie laughed a little ruefully. 'There was an awfully nice ski instructor, who picked me up and carried me back to the hotel. All the other girls were green with envy. He was quite a dish!'

Andreas's mouth was drawn into a compressed line now as he inclined his head in acknowledgement of her story, before rising abruptly to his feet. Sylvie suspected she had said too much, and that her conversation had begun to bore him, and impulsively she stood up, too, wishing she could think of something terribly clever and sophisticated to say. But of course she couldn't. She had simply dried up, and her thoughts were so chaotic that when he went to step past her she moved into his path instead of out of it. In consequence, the ribbed sole of his track shoe came down heavily on her bare toes, and she cried out instinctively as the pain increased.

Andreas realised what he had done at once and stepped back immediately, uttering a savage oath in his own language. '*Theos*, have I hurt you?' he muttered, grasping her by the shoulders, then shook his head self-derisively as she blinked back the betraying tears.

'It—it was my fault,' she got out, giving him a watery smile, but Andreas made a sound of denial.

'It was my fault,' he corrected her harshly, his hands on her shoulders clenching convulsively. He looked down at her half impatiently. 'Are you sure there are no bones broken?'

'I don't think so.' Sylvie lifted the injured foot and rubbed it experimentally against her other leg. 'No, honestly, it seems all right. I'm sorry I made such a fuss about it.'

'Nonsense!' Andreas's dark face still showed concern, and Sylvie, looking up at him, felt her senses suddenly quicken. For the first time he was looking at her as if he was really seeing her, and the awareness of the effect he had had on her earlier brought a becoming surge of colour to her face.

As if he had become aware of their proximity, too, Andreas's hands on her shoulders slackened. His touch through the thin cotton was no longer so aggressive, but she could still feel the steel in those long fingers.

'You are all right, then?' he demanded, his tone deepening unmistakably, and Sylvie nodded her head with a swift jerky motion.

'Thank you,' she breathed huskily, as that sensation that was neither a pleasure nor a pain flowered inside her again, and the moist scent of his body was suddenly strong in her nostrils.

'Sylvie——' he said unsteadily, and she thought he drew her slightly towards him, but then there was the sound of a key turning in the lock, and the outer door opened, and by the time Madame Kuriakis had entered the apartment, Andreas had put the width of the sofa between them.

Of course, nothing could alter the fact of Sylvie's state of undress, and the housekeeper looked slightly scandalised at the sight of her employer, evidently in conversation with his young guest. Perhaps she thought they had slept together, thought Sylvie wildly, still bemused by the events of the past few minutes, but when she turned to look at Andreas his face was withdrawn, the expression in his dark eyes as detached as ever. Had she imagined his sudden awareness? she wondered, her brow furrowing with the effort to gauge his thoughts. What had he really been thinking when he held her imprisoned within his hands? And what might have happened if Madame Kuriakis had not interrupted them, and destroyed so conclusively any intimacy between them?

The housekeeper spoke to Andreas in their own language, but Sylvie could sense no note of reproof in her words. It was only when Madame Kuriakis looked at her that she sensed the woman's hostility, and knew without a shadow of a doubt that the housekeeper blamed her for any impropriety that had occurred.

'I will go to shower and dress,' said Andreas in English, while the housekeeper started gathering the dirty teacups on to the tray. 'I shall be leaving in a little over an hour. If you would like me to give you a lift to my father's house, then I suggest you do the same.'

'All right.' Biting her lower lip rather anxiously, Sylvie followed him across the room, glancing over her shoulder at the stooped figure of the housekeeper. 'But oughtn't I to——'

'It is not your concern,' interrupted Andreas harshly, and as she passed him she encountered only a chilly politeness in his eyes, that bore no resemblance whatsoever to what she thought she had seen earlier.

Although it was barely nine o'clock, Leon was waiting for her when she arrived at the Petronides' mansion. He was seated in his wheelchair, in the wide entrance hall, and Sylvie's heart lightened at the sight of his welcoming face. It was good to know that at least one person wanted her here, she thought, and dismissed the contention that Leon could easily become too dependent on her. He was just a nice person, she told herself firmly, and kissed his pale cheek without further self-analysis.

Andreas had left her at the gates, saying he did not have the time to come in himself. He had hardly spoken during the fifteen-minute drive from the apartment to his parents' house, and although he had driven himself, in a sleek black sports saloon that Sylvie admired very much, his attitude had not encouraged any overtures from her. Since Madame Kuriakis's intervention he had become taciturn and almost morose, dismissing Sylvie's suggestion of telling

Marina they were leaving with the curt rejoinder that she could call for transport when she was ready. It was true Marina was not up, and Sylvie's tentative opening of her door had promoted nothing more dramatic than a sleepy groan from the bed, but Andreas's behaviour had bordered on the boorish, and Sylvie didn't know why. Surely he was not afraid of what Madame Kuriakis might say? Surely the opinions of his staff did not influence his actions? And besides, what was there to talk about? Nothing, so far as Sylvie was concerned.

But now Leon was smiling at her and asking if she had slept well, and banishing Andreas's image from her mind, Sylvie replied honestly that she had had a good night's rest. 'The bed was so comfortable,' she confided, taking charge of the wheelchair. 'Now, where is Nikos? I'm dying to see him.'

Nikos was waiting for them in the nursery. He was still sitting over his breakfast, one elbow propped on the table, supporting his head with one knuckled fist. He looked totally dejected, totally despondent, and Sylvie wondered again how Margot could neglect her son so.

A maid was standing to one side of him, urging him to eat some of the milky cereal set in front of him, but Nikos was not interested in it, or in the warm rolls in their dish. There was fresh fruit juice, too, and oranges and peaches, but the little boy was uninterested, and observing his thin arms and legs, Sylvie decided it was high time someone took him in hand.

'*Ghia*, Nikos!' his father greeted him cheerfully, as Sylvie pushed the wheelchair into the sunlit playroom. 'Here is Aunt Sylvie come to see you. And you still drooping over your breakfast!'

The little boy's head lifted, and he gazed across the room at his father and the girl behind him with some consternation. Dark curly hair framed a face that was an amalgam of both his father's and his uncle's, but softer, and gentler, and infinitely more poignant, with its haunted dark eyes and vulnerable mouth. He looked as if he had been crying, and Sylvie guessed Leon had spoken to him earlier, and told him his mother would not be coming. Poor Nikos, she thought; he would not understand why his mother had deserted him. No wonder Marina had hinted at his instability. He was obviously fretting over Margot's continued neglect.

'Until I was ill, he seemed quite content to accept his mother's absence,' Leon remarked to her now, in an undertone, echoing Sylvie's own sentiments. 'I had hoped that with the attention of both parents, he would learn to trust us again. I fear he is suffering the effects of insecurity, and even my parents cannot compensate for that.'

Sylvie nodded sympathetically, and then, leaving Leon to handle his own chair, she crossed the room to where Nikos and the maid were locked in silent combat. The maid stepped back politely as Sylvie bent down to her nephew, but Nikos still looked doubtful when she lightly touched his soft cheek.

'Do you remember me, Nikos?' she asked gently, pushing the unwanted dish of cereal aside. 'Do you remember coming to our house in Wimbledon, and me showing you all my dolls?'

Nikos hesitated a moment, then shook his head, but Sylvie refused to be daunted.

'Surely you do,' she persisted firmly. 'You played with my dolls. Don't you remember—one of them had hair that grew when you combed it? You liked that one. And the one that used to take its bottle and then wet its nappy.'

Nikos frowned. 'A doll that wet its nappy!' he echoed, in evident astonishment, and Sylvie giggled.

'That's right. Naughty, wasn't it?' she chuckled. 'So you do remember!'

'Not properly,' said Nikos solemnly. 'Was Mummy there?'

Sylvie sighed, glancing over her shoulder at Leon. 'Well, Mummy came with you,' she conceded at last. 'But you and I used to have lots of fun together.'

'Did we?' Nikos was unconvinced, and Sylvie took one of his hands in both of hers and squeezed tightly.

'Yes, we did,' she averred firmly. 'And what's more, we're going to have lots of fun now. Did Daddy tell you, we're going to spend a few weeks at the seaside? On an island called Monastiros. Do you know it?'

Nikos shook his head. 'Are you coming, too?'

'Try and stop me!' Sylvie smiled. 'I'm looking forward to it. We can swim—and make sand pies——'

'What are sand pies?' Nikos frowned again, and Sylvie looked appalled.

'Don't you know what sand pies are?' she exclaimed, and he shook his head. 'Well, you dig with your spade, and fill your bucket with damp sand, and when it's full, you turn it over.' She stared at him. 'Do you mean to tell me you've never made sand pies before?'

'Nikos is a little young to play alone on the beach,' Leon interposed, propelling himself towards them, and Sylvie straightened. 'And Dora was more concerned with health and hygiene than squatting on a beach playing childish games.'

'But you lived at the beach,' protested Sylvie, letting go of Nikos's hand to perch incredulously on the edge of the table.

'Alasyia is by the sea,' admitted Leon, 'but the ocean current is strong, and we have a swimming pool.'

'So you use that,' defined Sylvie flatly. 'Yes, I see.'

'There is no swimming pool on Monastiros,' Leon

added, with a wry smile. 'But you do not have to worry. The sea there is quite safe for swimming.'

'Good,' Sylvie grinned. 'A swimming pool is fun, but it's not half as much fun as the beach.'

Nikos slid off his seat and faced her, thin and a little pathetic, in his embroidered shirt and brief shorts. 'Do you mean that?' he asked. 'We really can play in the sand? I—I have never played on the beach before.'

'I promise,' said Sylvie firmly, bending to cup his pale little face between her hands. 'Now, have you got a kiss for Sylvie? You can call me that, if you like. *Aunt* Sylvie's much too formal for us.'

Nikos nodded shyly, offering his lips to hers, and Sylvie obliged, following the sweet salutation with a warm hug that, after a moment's hesitation, Nikos returned, with heart-warming eagerness. All he needed was love and attention, she thought, feeling a slight lump in her throat as she stepped back. Love and attention, from someone who cared.

CHAPTER FIVE

IT had been arranged that they should leave for Monastiros on Friday. A car would take them to the airport, and a helicopter would be waiting to transport them the hundred or so miles to their destination, one of the smaller islands in the group known as the Cyclades. Leon's valet, and the male nurse who had been looking after him, would accompany them, and his aunt Ariadne, would be waiting for them there. Apparently Leon's aunt lived on one of the adjacent islands, and would make the journey from her home to Monastiros by boat.

Leon divulged this information over lunch, which they took on the terrace at the back of the house, overlooking the sunlit waters of the swimming pool. Nikos was with them, but otherwise they were alone, Leon's father having departed for the office to join his eldest son, and his mother having a previous engagement. The two girls, Marina and Persephone, did not make an appearance, and Sylvie welcomed the opportunity to talk with Leon in private.

Nikos, who was still inclined to treat the proposed trip to the islands with a certain lack of conviction, grew quite animated at the prospect of flying in a helicopter, and questioned his father extensively about the flight and how long it would take. Watching Leon explain the answers to his son, Sylvie felt more relaxed than she had done for several days, and she began to anticipate the coming weeks with something more than apprehension. Leon was such a nice man, and she enjoyed his company, and for someone who had just suffered a serious operation, he was amazingly unconcerned about his own health. It was strange, but only now had Leon taken on a personality of his own. Until the day before, he had been Margot's husband, nothing more, but suddenly he was a person in his own right, and Sylvie found herself liking him more and more.

The car was summoned to take her back to Andreas's apartment after lunch. Nikos was taken away to have a nap, and Leon admitted that he, too, was obliged to rest during the long hot afternoons.

'Please come again tomorrow,' he urged her, as he bade her goodbye. 'Unless you'd prefer to go sightseeing. The Acropolis should not be missed.'

'I can see the Acropolis some other time,' averred Sylvie firmly, and his tired yet grateful image remained with her all the way back to the apartment.

Madame Kuriakis let her into the apartment, then disappeared about her own business. Sylvie, beginning to feel the effects of the heat, was glad to retire to her own room, and did not awaken until she heard someone knocking at her door.

'Sylvie?' called a youthful voice. 'Sylvie! It's Marina. Can I come in?'

'Oh—of course.'

Sylvie struggled up on her pillows, blinking in the shaft of sunlight that entered the room when the door was opened. She drew the silken coverlet up to her chin, having removed the cotton dress she had been wearing before she lay down, for although Marina was a young member of her own sex, she doubted she would feel comfortable seeing Sylvie half naked.

'*Kalispera*, Sylvie,' Marina greeted her smilingly, entering the room. 'I thought you might be awake. Would you like some tea? Madame Kuriakis is just making some.'

Sylvie smiled in return and nodded. 'I'd love a cup, thanks,' she accepted, running a rueful hand over the tangled length of her hair. 'Have I slept long? My watch appears to have stopped.'

'It is twenty-eight minutes after five o'clock,' said Marina precisely, after checking her own wrist. 'You must have been tired, Sylvie. Madame Kuriakis tells me you have been sleeping since three o'clock.'

Sylvie grimaced. 'Yes, I suppose I have.' She shrugged 'I got up quite early this morning. Perhaps it was too early.'

'Yes, I know.' Marina stood looking down at her, her hands linked demurely in front of her. 'You made yourself some tea, did you not? Madame Kuriakis told me.'

Sylvie chewed on her lower lip. 'Was she very cross? Madame Kuriakis, I mean. I was so thirsty, you see.'

'She was—surprised,' replied Marina cautiously. 'It is not usual for one of my brother's guests to prepare her own breakfast.'

'Oh, I didn't do that,' exclaimed Sylvie, shaking her head. 'I—I had a roll and some coffee later—with—with Andreas.' She paused, before adding: 'I don't think he was too pleased either.'

Marina made a moue. 'Andreas's guests are not usually female,' she remarked indifferently, and Sylvie knew an uneasy pang of excitement at the realisation that she would soon be seeing Andreas again. Perhaps he was already home, she thought, and her fingers tightened on the concealing coverlet. All day she had succeeded in keeping thoughts of him at bay, but Marina's casual words had rekindled her awareness of the feelings he had aroused inside her, and she couldn't wait to discover whether they had been the result of an overcharged imagination.

'Is—is your brother home?' she asked now, in what she hoped was a careless tone, then knew a momentary depression when Marina shook her head.

'Andreas is dining with a business associate this evening,'

she told Sylvie smilingly. 'But my brother Michael and his wife have invited us to dine with them, and afterwards they thought you might like to visit the Acropolis by moonlight.'

Sylvie squashed the sense of disappointment she was feeling, and forced a smile. 'That was very kind of them,' she answered formally, and Marina looked pleased.

'It is the least we can do, when you have been kind enough to come and look after Nikos,' she said. 'Now, put on your robe, and come and have some tea. Then we can discuss the arrangements for this evening.'

Over tea, Marina was disposed to gossip, and Sylvie heard all about Persephone's current boy-friend, whose family it appeared were not as well-to-do as the Petronides.

'Papa is so afraid we girls are married because of the money we expect to inherit, and not for ourselves,' she remarked, with wry candour. 'Christina and Diana are both married to the sons of other shipping families, so they are safe, but Persephone and myself must be constantly on our guard, particularly after—well,' she coloured slightly, 'you can understand, I am sure.'

'Leon,' said Sylvie dryly, and Marina looked a little discomfited.

'He has not had a happy marriage,' she admitted with a sigh, and Sylvie nodded.

Then, choosing her words carefully, she said: 'Hasn't Andreas ever wanted to get married? I mean—your other brothers are all married, aren't they?'

'Except Loukas,' Marina agreed, frowning. 'But Loukas is only nineteen. He is more interested in fast cars than fast women.' She giggled.

Sylvie put down her teacup, wondering how she could bring the conversation back to Andreas, but it was unnecessary. Marina did it for her, cradling her teacup between her hands, and gazing thoughtfully into space.

'Andreas was going to marry Eleni,' she said reflectively, and the muscles in Sylvie's stomach tightened unpleasantly. 'You know Eleni, do you not? You met her last evening.' And after Sylvie had nodded, she went on: 'But he waited too long, and she married someone else.'

'Eleni is married!' Sylvie couldn't prevent the instinctive exclamation, but Marina was already shaking her head.

'No longer,' she said regretfully. 'Her husband died last year. Eleni is a widow now, and since Giorgios's death, Andreas has been most attentive.'

Sylvie hesitated. 'And—and do you think he intends to marry her?' she ventured, with faint contempt at her own inquisitiveness, but Marina seemed not to notice.

'Who knows?' she said, with a shrug. 'Perhaps.' She turned teasing eyes in Sylvie's direction. 'Who knows what a man like Andreas will do? He is old enough to make his own decisions. Too old for you and me to understand his reasoning, I suspect.'

Sylvie bent her head. 'How—er—how old is he?' she asked, casually, reaching for her cup again, and Marina smiled.

'Thirty-four,' she said. 'He'll be thirty-five at the end of September. Why?' Her eyes danced. 'Do you find him attractive, too?'

Sylvie's colour deepened, but she didn't pretend to be indifferent. 'He's an attractive man,' she replied, giving the Greek girl a steady look. 'What girl wouldn't be aware of it?'

Marina grimaced. 'Well, do not let him hurt you, Sylvie.' She paused. 'Not that I think he would. He must appreciate, as we do, that he is much too old for you. And besides,' she moved her shoulders dismissingly, 'you are unlikely to see him again, once you leave for Monastiros.'

Sylvie slept less well that night, and it was the conversation she had had with Marina that kept her in that shallow state between sleeping and waking. The evening they had spent with Michael and his wife, Luci, had been very pleasant. After dinner they had driven up to the Acropolis, and Sylvie knew she would never forget the thrill of walking through the columns of the Propylaea or standing before the crumbling ruins of the Parthenon. It didn't matter that some of the buildings had had to be closed, owing to the effects of air pollution, or that the throng of tourists made a mockery of its sanctuary. It was still a magnificent example of architecture, over two thousand years old, and as awe-inspiring now as it had ever been.

Once again, Andreas had not been home when they arrived back at the apartment, and after sharing a pot of coffee, Sylvie and Marina had gone to bed. But not to sleep, so far as Sylvie was concerned. She was still awake when the lift came whining up to the penthouse floor of the apartment building, and she heard Andreas's key being inserted in the lock, and his eventual progress to his bedroom.

No doubt because of her disturbed night, she overslept the next morning, and by the time she had dragged herself out of bed and put her clothes on it was after nine o'clock. Examining her reflection in the mirror of the dressing table, Sylvie had to admit she looked as if she had had a heavy night, and her lips twisted wryly at this erroneous connotation. Dining with Andreas's brother and his wife had been enjoyable, but she couldn't help wondering if Andreas would have dined with his business associate if he had thought they would be on their own. It was a hypothetical question, and one which hardly deserved an answer. After all, it was not Andreas's task to entertain her, only to accommodate her, and he would probably rather not do that either, she reflected, with sudden perversity.

She spent the morning with Leon and Nikos again, Marina phoning for a car to take them to the Petronides house after they had had breakfast. Sylvie, expecting her to call a taxi, was sorry when Spiro arrived to escort them. Somehow, living in such a cloistered atmosphere, kept one apart from any real experience of Athens, but when she voiced her objections to Leon later he was quick to point out the advantages.

'Surely you would not dismiss the air-conditioned luxury of the Mercedes in favour of some ramshackle conveyance!' he protested. 'While it is my belief that Athens is one of the most beautiful cities in the world, I am not blind to its shortcomings, and I doubt you would really choose the garlic-scented breath of some old *taxitzis* to the comfort of a chauffeur-driven limousine.'

'At home, I should probably travel on the bus,' retorted Sylvie shortly, pushing her hands into the pockets of her jeans, which she had brought in spite of Margot's warning. 'Why couldn't we use public transport? I mean, aside from its evident lack of convenience, it is the only way to see the city.'

Leon smiled a little wryly. 'It has been my experience that such ideas generally do not achieve their objective. Do you think a Greek would not know that you were a stranger in his country? The way you look—the way you dress—these things all proclaim that you are not Greek——'

'What's wrong with the way I dress?' Sylvie was instantly defensive, and Leon laughed.

'Nothing, nothing,' he assured her warmly. 'Believe me, I like the way you look. I like your clothes, and I like the way your hair hangs, so smooth and straight. And I also like the way you are not afraid to speak up for yourself. This shows your independence.' He paused. 'But you must have noticed the differences between Marina and yourself. For instance, she would never dream of wearing trousers for an evening engagement, as you did two nights ago. I doubt if she possesses a pair of jeans, such as you are wearing now. Greek girls are more conservative in their dress—more——'

'—feminine?' suggested Sylvie tautly, and Leon laid a gentle hand on her arm.

'Of course not,' he averred, his eyes tender. 'You are a very feminine little lady, Sylvie, as I am sure you are aware. But it is this, as much as anything, which would set you apart.'

Sylvie sighed. 'You make me feel self-conscious.'

'That was not my intention,' Leon smiled. 'But do not doubt that you would attract attention, wherever you went, and believe me, that can be a most unpleasant experience.'

Sylvie nodded. 'I suppose you're right. I just wish——'

'What? That you could see more of my city?' Leon sighed. 'I wish I could show it to you.' His face darkened. 'Perhaps—one day.'

Sylvie bit her lip, feeling suddenly contrite. Here she had been bemoaning the fact that she wasn't being allowed the freedom to get about as she willed, while Leon had to listen to her, knowing the bitterness of his own limitations.

'I'm sorry,' she said impulsively. 'I wish you could show it to me, too. Perhaps, after your recuperation——'

'Perhaps,' agreed Leon, squeezing her arm before letting her go, and Sylvie determined not to be so selfish again.

To everyone's apparent astonishment, Andreas arrived at about one o'clock. Lunch was about to be served, on

the terrace as before, but this time Madame Petronides
and Persephone had joined them. The two Greek women
gazed at the newcomer with some perplexity, and his
mother's brow furrowed as Andreas bent to kiss her cheek.
Sylvie, watching him, thought what a marked contrast
there was between him and Leon. Although Andreas was
not heavily built, his lean body rippled with muscle, and
as he bent over the table, the buttons of his shirt strained
across his taut stomach. Leon, on the other hand, was all
skin and bone, with the angularity that came from prolonged illness. If only she could help him to recover, Sylvie
thought urgently, then what she was doing might be
proved worthwhile.

Andreas's eyes flickered round the table, resting for a
moment on her determined young face. His eyes,
narrowed against the glare of the sun, seemed to linger
longer than was necessary, Sylvie felt, still wrapped up in
her thoughts of devoting herself to Leon's recovery, and
although it couldn't possibly be so, he seemed to defy
her inner dedication. The fact that it seemed to find no
approval in his estimation aroused Sylvie's indignation,
but before she could exhibit her resentment, Nikos had
slid down from his seat and rushed round the table to his
uncle's side.

'Thios Andreas, Thios Andreas!' he exclaimed excitedly.
'Do you know what Sylvie says we are going to do? We are
going to make sand pies on the beach, and sand castles, and
paddle in the water, and even look for shells, if there are
rock pools!'

'One moment, Nikos.' Andreas stayed the boy's eager
chatter. 'Who gave you permission to call Aunt Sylvana
Sylvie?'

'I did,' said Sylvie immediately, her face a little pink
even so. 'Does it matter?' She glanced at Nikos's father.
'Leon doesn't mind.'

Andreas took the chair a servant had placed for him beside his mother, and held the boy between his knees. 'So——' he said, without answering her, 'you are happy now to be going to Monastiros, Nikos?'

'Oh, yes!' The little boy was eager, and after a few moments Andreas smiled at him.

'That is good. I am pleased. It will do you—good, I am sure.'

'You will come and visit us there, will you not, *thios*?' Nikos asked anxiously, and Sylvie waited with bated breath for Andreas's reply.

But it was Leon who answered his son, his tone faintly weary as the effort of maintaining a social attitude got the better of him. 'Of course he will, Nikos,' he retorted tiredly. 'Why should he not? It is his home, after all.'

Sylvie was still digesting this when the meal was over, and the various members of the family were dispersing about their own affairs. Leon's nurse had arrived to wheel him away for his rest, but before he left, he had the man propel his chair to Sylvie's side.

'We leave for the airport at eleven o'clock tomorrow morning,' he told her gently. 'This time tomorrow we will be arriving at the island. Nikos, I know, cannot wait, and I find I, too, grow more impatient by the minute.'

Sylvie smiled. 'Until tomorrow, then.'

'*Tha idhothoume avrio!*' Leon answered warmly, and as the male nurse wheeled him away, Andreas's shadow fell across the chair on which she was sitting.

'Come,' he said, without preamble. 'I will drive you back to the apartment.'

Sylvie caught her lower lip between her teeth. 'It's not necessary,' she said, even though her senses had automatically stirred at the sight of him. 'I—I believe Spiro is going to take me.'

'I will take you,' returned Andreas, putting his hand

beneath her elbow and levering her to her feet. 'Say fare-well to my mother. It may be some weeks before you see her again.'

Sylvie's jaw tightened, but she did as she was told, ap-proaching the older woman tentatively and offering her goodbyes. 'I'm sorry if my coming here has been a disap-pointment to you, *madame*,' she said, by way of an apology. 'I can only assure you I'll do everything I can to keep Nikos happy.'

Madame Petronides hesitated. 'So long as you ap-preciate that as soon as more satisfactory arrangements can be made, your services will not be required, *thespinis*,' she said succinctly, her dark eyes sharp with disapproval, and Sylvie caught her breath.

'You don't imagine I want to stay here indefinitely, do you, *madame*?' she exclaimed indignantly. 'I—I—am going to university in the autumn. Being Nikos's nursemaid is not the height of my ambitions, I can assure you!'

'I am pleased to hear it.' Madame Petronides was in-furiatingly tranquil. 'However, I have to say that your sister seemed more than ready to give up her ambitions to marry Leon, and you might consider a wealthy husband sufficient compensation for an uncertain future.'

Sylvie gasped. 'If you think that I am interested in Andreas, *madame*——'

'Andreas! *Andreas!*' Madame Petronides could not have looked more amused. 'My dear child, I have no fears of Andreas getting involved with someone so—unsuitable. No. No, I meant Leon, of course. He has already proved himself vulnerable.'

Sylvie was staring at her aghast, when Andreas, growing impatient at the delay, came to join them. 'You are ready?' he enquired, with cool interrogation, and Sylvie looked up at him indignantly before turning and walking away.

He caught up with her in the hall outside, his dark face contorted with anger. 'Is this how you repay my mother's hospitality?' he demanded. 'Do you not even acknowledge the food you have eaten at her table?'

'Right now, I would willingly throw up the food I've eaten at her table!' retorted Sylvie without refinement, and heard the muffled obscenity he tried to stifle. 'My God! Don't talk to me about hospitality! Your mother doesn't know the meaning of the word!'

Andreas's hard fingers caught her arm, bare below the sleeve of the thin cotton shirt she was wearing, and brought her to an abrupt halt. 'You will take that back!' he snapped savagely, but she just gazed up at him mutely, her lips pressed tightly together.

Andreas glared down at her for several charged seconds, and then, with another oath, he let her go, pacing beside her as she marched out of the house. His car, the sleek Ferrari she had travelled in the previous morning, was waiting outside, and without looking at him Sylvie opened the door and subsided into the bucket seat in silent defiance.

Even though the car had been parked in the shade with all the windows open, it was incredibly hot inside. However, as soon as Andreas had levered himself behind the wheel, he closed the windows and turned on the conditioning system, and in no time at all cool air was fanning Sylvie's hot cheeks. He had shed his jacket, tossing it into the back of the car as he got in beside her, and she could see the fine silk of his shirt sticking to him in places. In the confined intimacy of the car, she was intensely conscious of him, and of his anger, and although she told herself her outburst had been justified, she doubted he would ever forgive her for defying him in this way.

The hot tires spun on the gravel of the drive as Andreas turned the car with suppressed violence and drove towards the gates. They swung open automatically for him, then they were out in the quiet, tree-shaded avenue, accelerating down the sweating road.

They drove in silence for some distance, a silence Sylvie would have willingly broken now if she could have thought of something relevant to say. But short of offering an apology, which she had no intention of doing, she doubted he would answer her, and she felt too strung up to suffer any further humiliation.

At last Andreas slowed the car to a more civilised pace, and turning to glance at her said coldly: 'Suppose you tell me what provoked that exhibition of juvenile insolence just now. I have come to the conclusion that there must have been a reason for your childish display.'

'Oh, have you?' His patronising words rekindled Sylvie's sense of injustice. 'Well, don't let me be the one to shake your faith in your mother. Forget it. Come tomorrow, I'll be out of your hair.'

Then she remembered what Leon had said about Monastiros being Andreas's home, and hunched her shoulders. What did it mean? That they would be living in Andreas's house? After this little interlude she hoped not.

'I want to know what my mother said to you,' Andreas was insisting harshly, and Sylvie cupped her chin on one hand and turned to stare out of the window. 'I mean to know, Sylvana. One way or the other, you are going to tell me.'

'Oh, for heaven's sake!' Sylvie was suddenly very near to tears, and she sniffed with unknowing emphasis. 'What does it matter what she said? She doesn't like Margot, and she doesn't like me. That's all there is to it!'

Andreas swore softly, and stepped on his brakes, bringing the Ferrari to a smooth halt on a knoll, overlooking a stretch of wooded parkland. The greenery was a soothing contrast to the dazzling whiteness of the buildings in the distance, and nearer at hand a fountain played coolly into a stone basin. At this hour of the afternoon it was very quiet, very peaceful, but Sylvie did not feel at peace when Andreas turned in his seat to face her.

'Now,' he said, 'your explanation please. As quickly as possible.'

'I'm not a child, you know,' Sylvie retorted mutinously, lifting her shoulders against him.

'Then stop behaving like one,' he advised her shortly, running two fingers inside his collar. 'Why were you so rude? What did Mama say?'

Sylvie pursed her lips. 'Mama——' and she gave his mother's name unnecessary emphasis, '*Mama* said——'

'Go on!'

'—well,' Sylvie's defiance was rapidly deserting her, 'she said I shouldn't imagine my position was a permanent one.'

'Your position?'

'Yes.' Sylvie sighed. 'You know—looking after Nikos. She said that as soon as more satisfactory arrangements could be made, my services would not be required.'

Andreas's mouth turned down at the corners. 'And this angered you?' he asked disbelievingly. 'I thought it was what you wanted—the opportunity to leave as soon as possible.'

Sylvie's mouth worked silently. 'Well—yes. Yes, it was. It *is*! But not like that.'

'Not like what?' he asked, his impatience with her answers growing evident, and Sylvie sniffed again.

'All right,' she said defensively. 'All right, I'll tell you what she said. She said I shouldn't get ideas. Is that what you want to hear?'

'Ideas?' Andreas looked suspicious now. 'What kind of ideas.'

Sylvie sighed. 'Ideas—about Leon.'

'Leon!' Andreas made an impatient gesture. 'Sylvana, either I am not understanding what you are saying, or you are not explaining yourself very well. Which is it?'

She hesitated. 'She—she thinks I might get ideas about how pleasant it would be to be married to Leon myself.'

'You cannot be serious!' Andreas's face was dark with anger now as he stared at her.

'Why not?' Sylvie shrugged. 'That's what your mother said. She suspects I might become addicted to the idea of having a rich husband.'

Andreas's mouth compressed. 'And what did you tell her?'

Sylvie's eyes widened. 'I denied it, of course.' Then, deliberately, watching his reaction, she added: 'I thought she meant you at first.'

'Me?' Andreas's hand went up to his tie, and with a jerk, he pulled the knot down below his collar. 'Why should you think that?' he asked, his eyes narrowed and hostile, and Sylvie hastily withdrew her offensive.

'Oh, I don't know, do I? I suppose, with Leon already being married——'

'Yes. Yes, he is, is he not?' Andreas looked strangely remote suddenly. 'Perhaps you would do well to remember that.'

Sylvie gasped. 'You mean you agree with her?'

Andreas swore softly. 'I did not say that.'

'You didn't have to.' Sylvie forgot her fears in the face of his condoning of his mother's behaviour. 'How can you even suggest such a thing? Leon is your brother! He's been very ill. Just because I show him some—some concern, some—affection, must you spoil it all by suggesting I have some ulterior motive?'

'I did not say that,' declared Andreas harshly. 'Do not be so damned sensitive, Sylvana! Try to remember, it is over a year since Leon and Margot lived together. He is only human, and you are here. Margot is not.'

Sylvie drew an unsteady breath. 'I think that's a foul thing to suggest!'

'Why?' Lines bracketed Andreas's mouth as he looked at her. 'I can tell by the way he looks at you, the way he speaks to you, that he finds your company—sympathetic.'

Sylvie found she was trembling. She didn't know why. She only knew that being with Andreas disturbed her in a way that was essentially dangerous—dangerous, because his presence stimulated her imagination in a way that was at once thrilling and shocking. With him, her body responded instinctively to his physical attraction, but although she might fantasise about his kisses, she had few doubts that she would find the reality terrifying. Andreas was not Brian, he was nothing like Brian, and what was more, he was a man, whereas Brian was only a boy.

'What is the matter?'

He had become aware of her sudden agitation, and Sylvie shook her head in mute denial, as his dark brows drew closer together. 'N-nothing,' she stammered, looking away from him, out of the open window of the car, but he was not satisfied with her answer, and his long fingers curved round her jawline, turning her face back to him.

'Sylvana?' he said, frowning, and her troubled expression must have given him an answer, because his lips parted in angry comprehension. '*Theé mou*, there is no need to look at me like that! You can trust Leon. He will not hurt you. He is in need of—consolation, that is all. If you wish, I will speak to him——'

'*No!*' Frustratedly, Sylvie dashed his hand away from her chin, stung by his lack of perception, even though half of her breathed more freely for his misunderstanding. 'Leave me alone, can't you? And leave Leon alone, too. He doesn't need you, and nor do I!'

'You go too far!' Andreas's face was contorted with anger, and Sylvie had to steel herself not to shrink back against the door. For an awful moment she thought he intended to strike her, and her palsied limbs suffered a slight paralysis. But then, with a gesture of contempt, whether at her or at himself she could not be sure, he controlled the impulse, raking his scalp with agitated fingers, ruffling the normally smooth swathe of dark hair. Resting his elbows on the steering wheel, he sat like that for a few moments before reaching automatically for the ignition, and Sylvie's galloping heartbeat slowed to a fast tattoo.

'Andreas ...' She heard herself say his name as he reached for his keys, a tremulous indication of her own trepidation. 'Andreas—please, I'm sorry. I shouldn't have said what I did.'

He turned to look at her then, the dark eyes raking her face, as his nails had raked his scalp only minutes before. 'You are sorry,' he echoed harshly. 'And what am I supposed to say?'

Sylvie drew an unsteady breath. 'You're—you're not *supposed* to say anything. I—I just wanted to—apologise. For speaking too impulsively.'

'Impulsively?' His dark eyes were full of scorn. 'Do you not mean indiscreetly?—recklessly?—*foolishly*, even?'

'If you like.' Sylvie moved her shoulders helplessly.

'If *I* like!' Andreas expelled his breath derisively. 'You expect me to believe this nonsense!'

'It's not nonsense.' Sylvie sighed. 'I don't want to quarrel with you, Andreas. I don't want to quarrel with anyone.' She paused. 'I didn't start this, you know.'

Andreas surveyed her anxious expression without sympathy, and Sylvie felt the hopelessness of knowing she had transgressed beyond the bounds of common civility. If only she hadn't let his mother's words upset her, she thought, none of this need have happened.

The silence stretched between them, and again, acting on impulse, Sylvie said: 'Couldn't we walk for a while? I mean, I suppose you have to get back to the office soon, and all that, but couldn't we just try and be pleasant with one another?'

Andreas's dark brows descended. 'Are you not tired? Do you not wish to rest? The heat——'

'Oh, I'm all right.' Sylvie gave him a pleasing smile. 'I don't need to rest. Do you?'

Andreas's expression softened slightly. 'You mean because of my great age, I suppose,' he mocked, and she shook her head indignantly, the heavy strands of her hair folding on her shoulders.

'No,' she denied vehemently. 'You're not old.' Her lips parted. 'Are you trying to start another argument?'

'Perhaps,' remarked Andreas dryly. 'Perhaps it is safer.' And with this cryptic comment he closed the car windows and thrust open his door.

It was very hot when Sylvie stepped out into the sunshine, but the heat had never troubled her. The thickness of her hair was sufficient covering for her head, and its length successfully protected the more vulnerable skin at her nape. She waited while Andreas locked the car, but when he would have tightened the knot of his tie, her hand on his sleeve stopped him.

'Don't you ever relax?' she asked, as he resisted her efforts to stay him, and with a shrug of his shoulders he let his hand fall, leaving the knot where it was.

They walked across the grass, Sylvie very conscious of his tall frame beside her. His leanness, too, made her overly aware of the rounder contours of her body, and she wondered if he had any objections to the tight-fitting jeans. Still, at least there were few people about to observe their progress, and she relaxed after a while and spread her arms wide.

'Hmm, isn't the sun wonderful!' she exclaimed, feeling its heat already burning her creamy flesh. 'I like winters, you know. I like sledging and skiing, and toasting chestnuts over an open fire, but summer has so much more to offer. Don't you think?'

Andreas moved his shoulders in a casual gesture, neither acknowledging nor denying her statement, and as she pondered the proposition that he might still be angry with her Sylvie's exuberance faltered. She had hoped that once they were out of the car his anger would be forgotten, but judging by the serious expression he was wearing, he had not forgiven her earlier indiscretions.

She halted in the shade of a clump of orange trees, the scent of their blossom mingling with that of the flowering shrubs, which grew in such profusion. It was very pleasant in the shade, with only the distant hum of the traffic and the buzzing of the insects to disturb the stillness. She stopped beside one of the trees and leant her shoulders back against the bark, and Andreas, forced to halt also, stopped just in front of her.

Sylvie schooled herself to meet his gaze steadily, and then, with determined candour, she asked: 'Are you still angry with me?'

Andreas did not immediately reply, but when he did, his tone was clipped: 'I suppose not.'

'Good.' Sylvie decided to accept him at his word, however reluctant he had been to voice it. 'I'm glad. I don't like being out of friends with people.' She paused, then added sturdily: 'Particularly people I like.'

Andreas's response to this was a wry twisting of his lips, before placing one hand on either side of her on the bole of the tree. 'You do not know me, Sylvana,' he declared dryly. 'How can you know if you like me?'

Sylvie's skin prickled at his nearness, but she managed to hide her consternation as she replied: 'I do know you.

I've known you for seven years. We met at Margot's wedding. And—and I wish you wouldn't keep calling me Sylvana!'

'Very well—Sylvie! You knew me so well, you did not even recognise me at the airport.'

Sylvie flushed. This was going on longer than she had expected, and while she was glad his antagonism had been averted, she was increasingly troubled by the knowledge that his nearness was causing a distinct constriction in her breathing, and the unwelcome awareness of moisture breaking out all over her body.

'That—that was different,' she managed to say now. 'I was expecting to see Leon. You know I was. And you—well, you looked so aggressive!'

Andreas's lips twisted. 'I *was* aggressive,' he confirmed, taking his hand from the bark to lift one of the thick strands of hair that lay over her shoulder. Smoothing it between his finger and thumb, he went on softly: 'I had had my suspicions that Margot might not fufil her obligations. When I saw you, I knew I had been right.'

Sylvie's breasts were heaving, and looking down, she saw their fullness outlined against the thin material of her shirt. Her excitement was evident, and she glanced up anxiously, half afraid that Andreas might notice, and found his attention focussed in the same place. Their eyes met, then moved swiftly away, and Andreas stepped back, releasing her hair and removing his other hand from the bole of the tree.

'We should go back to the car,' he said, his jaw clenched tautly, and Sylvie nodded. 'You are all right?' he added huskily, as she swayed when she straightened away from the tree.

'I think so,' she breathed, unknowingly provocative with that slightly bemused look in her eyes, and Andreas was suddenly very close. In the space of a second his hand had slid behind her nape, his thumb tilting her face up to his, and before she could utter any words of protest, he had covered her mouth with his.

A wave of panic swept over her at the touch of his lips, but his kiss was so persuasive, she was instantly disarmed. His mouth was not heavy or frightening, as she had expected, but gentle and beguiling, winning her confidence, and causing her to respond to him with tentative ardour. When his tongue rubbed against her lips, warm and moist and intimate, she gave an involuntary shiver, for its sensuous exploration was infinitely more disturbing than Brian's usually forceful approach had been. It made her aware of herself, aware of him, and aware of the muscled pressure of his body, compelling her back against the tree.

Sylvie had never experienced anything like the feelings he was arousing in her. She wanted to arch herself against him, to mould her body to his, to feel his weight crushing her against the tree behind her. Her lips parted helplessly, powerless to resist him, and as his mouth opened to accommodate hers, the tenor of the embrace significantly deepened.

What had begun as a salutary caress became a suffocating assault on her emotions, and the mindless rapacity of her senses responded instinctively to the urgency of his. In a fleeting moment of coherency she thought perhaps he had not intended it to go so far, but she could not fight against the wild hunger he had inspired, and her hands clung to the hair at the nape of his neck. He was all feeling, breathing male at that moment, demanding and taking the sweetness of her mouth, with a mastery that both excited and devastated her.

The embrace ended when the blast of a car horn in the distance brought Andreas to an awareness of where he was and what he was doing. The realisation seemed to galvanise him. With a groan of anguish he put his hands against the bole of the tree and pushed himself away from her, regarding her quivering recovery with frustrated eyes. Then, with a gesture of contempt directed solely at himself, he shook his head.

Sylvie looked back at him with eyes still glazed by her response to his lovemaking. She was finding it incredibly hard to restore her composure, and her pale cheeks and bruised lips bore witness to the ardent possession of his mouth.

'Are you all right?' asked Andreas, after a moment, and indicated the way back to the car. 'Shall we go?' he added, his voice clipped and constrained, and with a jerky nod Sylvie propelled herself away from the comparative support of the tree.

Her legs felt abysmally weak, and scarcely capable of performing the function for which they were provided, but somehow she made herself follow him, and was rewarded by his brooding look of approval.

Having settled her into her seat, Andreas walked round the car to join her, but after levering his length behind the wheel, he did not immediately reach for the ignition.

'I know I should apologise,' he said, in a low tone, staring straight in front of him. 'I had no right to—do what I did, and what is more to the point, I should have had more sense!'

'More sense!' Sylvie drew an uneven breath. 'Didn't you want to kiss me?'

Andreas looked sideways at her. 'That question is not worthy of an answer,' he replied, and then looked ahead again. 'I am a man. I took advantage of your youth.'

Sylvie allowed her breath to escape on a small sigh. 'There's no need to apologise,' she said, rapidly gaining control of herself again, and he turned his head.

'Perhaps you do not deserve it,' he declared harshly. 'Perhaps because you are a provocative young lady you do not expect any apology from me. But I am a Greek. I have certain—codes that I live by. And getting involved with acquisitive teenagers is not one of them.'

Sylvie knew she should object to his description of her as an acquisitive teenager, but his comment that she was a provocative young lady was so novel, she could think of nothing else. He actually thought she was provocative! She clasped her hands together and pressed them to her chest. Life was certainly becoming more interesting, when in the space of ten days she had been described as 'sexy' and 'provocative', particularly as her opinion had led her to believe just the contrary.

Hardly aware of the aggravation of her question, she turned to him shyly and widened her eyes. 'Do you really think I'm provocative?' she asked, seeking his confirmation, and with a muttered expletive Andreas started the car.

'My mother is right,' he stated grimly, thrusting the car into drive and accelerating savagely. 'Your looking after Nikos is an unsuitable arrangement—I realise that now. And as soon as I can find a replacement, you may return to London.'

Sylvie shrugged, but she did not take offence, even though the idea of returning to England was not at all appealing. She knew his angry reaction stemmed from the fact that he did find her provocative, and while later she might feel apprehensive of this new development, right now it was a tantalising prospect.

CHAPTER SIX

SYLVIE walked up the beach towards the villa, squeezing the salty water out of her hair. It was barely seven o'clock, but the sun was already warm on her shoulders, the water only several degrees lower than the eighty or so it generated in the middle of the day. She had taken to swimming at this hour every morning, and she looked with some approval at the golden tan she had already acquired. In spite of all the odds, she was enjoying herself, and what was more important, Leon and Nikos were happy, too.

Her brother-in-law looked much different now from the wan individual he had been on their arrival ten days ago. Then, he had been exhausted by the flight from Athens, and Stephanos, his nurse, and Paul, his valet, had practically had to lift him out of the helicopter and into the limousine, which had been waiting to drive them the short distance to the villa. After all, Leon had been convalescing since he left the hospital, and the strain of the journey had taken its toll.

But that was all in the past now. Several days of lying on the flagged patio outside the villa had removed the pallor of illness from his skin, and the peace and beauty of their surroundings were rapidly restoring him to health. His appetite had improved. He was gaining weight. And last evening he had even left his chair and walked with Sylvie down to the beach.

She remembered she had not wanted him to go. She had been afraid he might be trying to do too much. But Leon had only scoffed at the fears voiced by Sylvie and his aunt, and in all honesty, it didn't seem to have done him any harm.

Nikos had followed his father's example, and he, too, was well content. He had lost that uncertain look he had had that day at his grandfather's house, and free from all restraint, he was more than a match for his young aunt's energies.

Much to Sylvie's relief, Leon's aunt Ariadne was nothing like Madame Petronides. The old lady was his father's sister, and although she was not a talkative person, she had a gentle and sometimes humorous disposition that made their relationship seem totally natural. She was an adequate chaperon, if such a thing was needed, but she didn't intrude, and she was invariably to be found sitting on the balcony outside her bedroom, crocheting some of the intricate lace which was a characteristic craft of the islands. Leon had told Sylvie that the man his aunt had been going to marry had died during the German occupation, and that since then she had lived in isolation on Thirbos, another of the offshore islands.

Monastiros itself was a place of exquisite beauty, and Sylvie could still not quite believe the view that met her startled gaze every morning. The villa they were occupying was situated just above the bleached sands of a small cove, and two stone steps gave access to a sun-baked patio. Stone flags were set about with tubs of hibiscus and geraniums, that spilled their luscious blossoms with careless abundance, and it was here that they generally took their meals, overlooking the dazzling waters of the Aegean.

The villa itself was large, but not elaborate. Simply built of stone, and painted a brilliant white both inside and out, it sprawled at the foot of the gorse-shrubbed hills that rose in gentle terraces behind it. Its rooms were bare but spacious, furnished comfortably, but not luxuriously, with hand-made wooden furniture and locally woven carpets and rugs. It had a certain elegance, evidenced in the grand piano that graced a window embrasure, but its tasteful styling and plain symmetry fitted in well with the other dwellings dotted about the island. As well as the large living room, and the dining room which could be used on cooler days and in winter, there were six bedrooms and three bathrooms with a self-contained apartment attached to the kitchen at the back, where Irene and Stavros, the middle-aged couple who looked after the villa and its guests were accommodated. There was electricity, a luxury Sylvie had discovered not all of the islanders enjoyed, and a telephone connection with the mainland, which Leon explained his father had installed when his children were young, and he used to spend holidays here. It also explained why Leon had told Nikos the island was Andreas's home, too. The villa belonged to the family. They were all equally entitled to use it.

However, at present only the four of them were in residence, and remembering Andreas's attitude towards her before she left for Monastiros, Sylvie doubted anyone else would join them. The only reason Andreas might have for coming to the island would be to tell her he had found her replacement, and she refused to consider this when she was enjoying herself so much. If she occasionally permitted thoughts of that disturbing encounter in the park to enter her mind, they were never allowed to remain long. Exciting though it had been, that interlude with Andreas was unlikely to be repeated, and she thought it was just as well in the circumstances. Remembering how helpless she had been in his arms, she had decided she had had a lucky escape, and she had been quite glad to leave the apartment, and the inevitable intimacy of sharing his life. Besides, during her conversations with Leon she had learned that there was every reason to suppose that Andreas would be marrying Eleni in the not-too-distant future. His father wanted him to marry. He wanted more grandsons to carry on the family name. And Andreas was his eldest son.

Sylvie came up the steps to the terrace now, twisting her hair into a silky rope that lay over one shoulder. In her brief cotton bikini she looked long-limbed and golden, the very essence of youthfulness and ripening womanhood. To the man seated in the shade of the wall of the house she was the most delightful creature he had ever seen, and he rose automatically to greet her, eager to feel the warmth of her smile upon him.

'*Kalimera, aghapiti mou*,' he said, his voice evidently startling her, and Sylvie turned to him in surprise, acknowledging his welcome appearance.

'Leon!' she exclaimed, halting abruptly, surveying his briefly-clad body with wide amber eyes. 'But why aren't you resting? It's only seven o'clock! I thought, after last night, you'd be tired this morning.'

Leon smiled, brushing his bare legs below the cuffs of his shorts with some self-consciousness. 'I know—I look pale and insipid,' he said dryly. 'But I will tan, I assure you, and in a few weeks, who knows? I may yet join you in the water.'

'You look fine.' Sylvie was indignant, then she shook her head, and gestured behind him at the chair where he had been sitting. 'But do sit down again now. I have to go and take a shower and get changed. We can have breakfast together when I get back. I'll look forward to it.'

'Will you, Sylvie?' Leon watched her intently. 'So shall I.' He paused. 'And as it happens, I've ordered breakfast for us already.' He glanced behind him. 'Here it comes. Your shower must wait.'

Sylvie sighed, looking down at her damp body. Oh, well, she thought inconsequently, she could get a shower later. Right now it was enough to know that Leon felt well enough to join her at the breakfast table.

Irene the housekeeper brought the tray and set it on the glass-topped table, smiling benevolently at her master and his young guest. She spoke to him shyly in his own language, obviously asking him how he was and complimenting him on his evident improvement. Leon thanked her and smiled, while he watched Sylvie seating herself at the table with vaguely proprietorial eyes. The direction of his interest was not lost on the sharp-eyed Irene, and Sylvie would have been somewhat alarmed if she had heard the housekeeper regaling Stavros, her husband, with her conclusion as to the reasons for Kirios Leon's steady recovery.

'How are you really feeling this morning?' Sylvie asked, as Leon seated himself beside her and accepted the glass of freshly-squeezed orange juice she had poured. 'Don't— well, don't overdo it, will you?'

'Do not overdo what?' teased Leon, his eyes twinkling, and she coloured becomingly.

'You know!' she insisted refusing to repeat herself, and Leon's lips curved with satisfaction as he surveyed the picture she made.

'I will not,' he assured her now, 'but I felt so well this morning, and when I saw you in the water——' He paused. 'I wanted to be with you.'

Sylvie sighed. 'The sea is delicious at this hour of the morning,' she agreed, buttering a warm roll with mouth-watering anticipation. 'I would like to buy a snorkel, if I could learn how to use it. I swam underwater for quite some way just now, but the salt water stings my eyes, and goggles might give more protection.'

'Perhaps.' Leon was noncommittal, helping himself to some apricot conserve. 'But take care. I should not like you to swim out too far.'

'It's quite safe,' declared Sylvie, her voice muffled as she munched. 'And if I did get into difficulties, there are always fishermen I could hail.'

'Nevertheless, I wish you to take more care,' said Leon quietly, covering her hand with his where it lay on her knee, and she was nodding in obedience when a dark shadow fell across the table.

'So—am I interrupting something?' demanded harsh male tones, and Sylvie lifted her head disbelievingly to see Andreas profiled against the sun. His face was in shadow, so she could not read his expression, but his tall frame was unmistakable, and his tone was sufficient for her to know that he was not pleased by what he was witnessing.

Sylvie's instinctive impulse to snatch her hand from beneath Leon's was forestalled by his immediate reaction. With an exclamation of welcome he rose to his feet, and the two brothers embraced one another with genuine warmth.

'What are you doing here?' Leon exclaimed, after their initial greetings were over, speaking in English for Sylvie's benefit. 'How did you get here? We did not hear the helicopter.'

'I came on the overnight steamer from Piraeus, and walked up from the harbour,' replied Andreas casually, and as he moved round the table to take the seat Leon offered, Sylvie saw that he was more informally dressed than she had ever seen him. Instead of an expensive suit and immaculate linen, he was wearing a sweat-shirt and jeans, with a black leather jerkin draped over one shoulder. As he sat down, he dropped the jerkin on top of the haversack lying at his feet, and looking at him, Sylvie guessed his attire was deliberate. No one, seeing him for the first time, with an overnight growth of beard on his chin, would imagine he was the heir to the Petronides shipping chain, and like this he could travel incognito, untroubled by threats of violence or kidnapping.

'It was easy enough to take the ferry,' he continued, his eyes flickering thoughtfully over Sylvie's scantily-clad form. 'And I thought I would surprise you by arriving unannounced.'

'Well, you have certainly done that,' remarked Leon goodnaturedly. 'As you can see, we are hardly dressed for visitors. But Sylvie has been swimming, and I persuaded her to have breakfast with me, before she went to change.'

'So I see.' Andreas's dark eyes moved to Sylvie again, and her appetite disappeared completely beneath the mocking appraisal. 'How are you, Sylvie? Our climate appears to be agreeing with you. You are getting quite a tan.'

'Yes, I am, aren't I?' Sylvie wondered what he was really thinking. Did he imagine she and Leon did this every morning? Would he believe her if she told him it was not so?

'And you, Leon?' Andreas gave her some respite, and turned to his brother. 'Are you really feeling much better? You are not overtaxing yourself?'

'You are like Sylvie,' declared Leon impatiently. 'She is always so concerned that I do not do too much.'

'She is right,' said Andreas approvingly. 'You know what Maxwell said—a little progress at a time.'

'I—er—I'll go and tell Irene you're here,' said Sylvie abruptly, getting up from her seat, then sighing in embarrassment when both men rose also. 'Please—sit down. Go on with your conversation. I'll explain to Irene that—that we have another guest.'

'One moment.' Andreas bent to the haversack at his feet, and while Sylvie waited with some apprehension, he produced a handful of letters from inside. 'There are two for you—Sylvie,' he remarked rifling through them swiftly and producing the letters in question. 'As I needed the break, I thought I could deliver them in person.'

'Thank you.' Sylvie took the letters from him, and Leon, after a gesture of apology that preceded his retreat into his chair, said rather breathlessly: 'You are staying, then, Andreas?'

'For a few days,' Andreas conceded, his concern for his brother superseding his apparent desire to observe Sylvie's every reaction. '*Yia to Theo*, Leon, are you sure you should get up so early? Maxwell said you needed to rest.'

'Yes, you should be in bed, Leon.' Sylvie went swiftly to him, squatting down beside him and looking up at him with anxious eyes. 'Shall I ask Stephanos to bring the wheelchair? Or can I help you back to your room?'

'*No pari o thiavolos*, Andreas! I am all right.' Leon looked up at his brother as he put his hand on Sylvie's damp head in a revealingly possessive gesture. Then, as he transferred his attention to the girl, his expression grew gentle. 'Honestly, little one, I am fine. Just a little tired from standing, that is all. Go, speak with Irene. I am sure Andreas is just too polite to tell us he is dying of thirst.'

Sylvie's smile was only for him, and careless of what interpretation Andreas might put on her actions, she removed Leon's hand from her head and kissed his knuckles before replacing it on his knee. 'All right,' she said, 'I'll tell her. Then I'll go and take my shower before Nikos makes his appearance.'

Leon nodded, their mutual understanding evident in that small exchange, and without looking at Andreas again, Sylvie walked swiftly across the patio, aware of his eyes following her and registering her progress. The fact that he was staying was something she had yet to come to terms with, but at least he had not brought her replacement, and perhaps she should be thankful for that.

In her bedroom, she stripped off the damp bikini, then perched naked on the end of her bed to read her letters.

She had recognised the handwriting as her mother's and Margot's, and she wondered if Andreas's decision to give her the letters as she was leaving the table indicated that he knew Margot had written to her, too.

She opened her mother's letter first, unconsciously putting off reading Margot's, and quickly scanned Mrs Scott's scrawling handwriting. She had written to her mother before she left for Monastiros, explaining as much of the situation as she thought was necessary, and now her mother was writing back, expressing her concern that Leon's illness should have been kept from them. *They really should have let Margot know*, she wrote, and Sylvie sighed in exasperation as she realised her mother had misinterpreted her communication. In her efforts not to cause her mother any unnecessary anxiety, she had endeavoured to excuse Margot's behaviour by intimating that her sister could not have known how serious Leon's condition was, and Mrs Scott, ever ready to defend her elder daughter, had immediately assumed Margot hadn't been told the truth.

The rest of the letter was concerned with affairs at home—her mother's involvement in the youth festival, and her continuing success at bridge. She hardly mentioned Margot, which meant she hadn't seen her, and about Sylvie's own involvement she maintained a discreet silence.

Margot's letter was shorter, but equally self-centred. After expressing her relief that Sylvie was coping so well, she went on to say that rehearsals for the play were going well, and she was reasonably satisfied with her performance. *Gerry is having a few problems finding backers for the play*, she conceded, in one of her more candid statements, *but money is so tight everywhere it's hardly surprising, and he's firmly convinced that once they see the play, they'll be falling over themselves to support us.*

Sylvie was not so sure. Margot believed what she

wanted to believe. She always had. But, conversely, and rather selfishly, she knew, Sylvie half hoped the play would succeed. In spite of her reluctance to come here, she had settled down now, and the idea of leaving seemed remote and disagreeable.

When she emerged from the villa some thirty minutes later, after using a hand-drier on her hair, she was relieved to find only her nephew taking his breakfast on the patio. He raised his face obediently for her kiss, and then, continuing to fork slices of fresh melon into his mouth, he endeavoured to speak to her.

'Thios Andreas is here!' he announced, speaking with his mouth full in his excitement. 'Did you know? He came on the steamer before I woke up.'

Sylvie adjusted the halter straps of her cotton sundress and started to gather together the used dishes on the table. 'Yes,' she said, without enthusiasm, clattering the dishes. 'He arrived while I was having breakfast.'

'Did he?' Nikos looked up at her consideringly. 'You do not sound very pleased.' He frowned. 'Is something wrong? Do you not like Thios Andreas?'

Sylvie sighed, and moved her shoulders in a dismissing gesture. 'I neither like nor dislike him, Nikos. I hardly know him.'

She crossed her fingers on the lie, but Nikos was still looking at her with obvious speculation. 'Why are you wearing a dress?' he asked, wrinkling his nose. 'You do not usually wear dresses, Sylvie. Are you not going to play with me today?'

'Of course I am, silly.' Sylvie could not entirely keep the evidence of tension out of her voice. 'Can't I wear a dress if I feel like it? Don't you like it? Doesn't it suit me?'

Nikos shrugged. 'The dress is all right—I suppose,' he conceded grudgingly. 'But I like you better when you're not all dressed up.'

Sylvie glared at him impatiently, and had hardly squashed her amusement when the sound of footsteps on the stone flags made her glance round. Andreas was walking across the terrace towards them. He, too, had taken the time to change, and shave the overnight shadow from his chin, and beneath the frayed cuffs of his denim shorts his long legs were brown and muscular. The shorts were all he was wearing, and Sylvie looked away quickly from the sight of his torso, with its disturbing triangle of body hair arrowing down to his navel.

Fortunately, Nikos erased the tension of the moment by jumping down from his chair and going to meet his uncle, grinning up at him cheerfully, evidently glad to see him. For a few moments they spoke together in Greek, Andreas tolerantly correcting his nephew's somewhat erratic use of the language, and then, glancing at Sylvie, he bade the boy use English.

'We must not be rude in front of your aunt, Nikos,' he said, as his eyes met Sylvie's. 'It appears both you and your father have much to thank her for.'

'Oh, yes!' Nikos was enthusiastic. 'Me and Sylvie have had lots of fun.'

'Sylvie and I,' corrected Andreas dryly, and Sylvie fixed him with a deliberately mocking stare.

'Have we?' she teased, in faintly malicious tones, and once again it was Nikos who rescued the conversation.

'How long are you staying, Thios Andreas?' he asked, paying little attention to their double-talk. 'Are you here for a holiday? Is 'Leni coming? Can I show you how to build a castle on the beach?'

Andreas made a quelling gesture. 'All in good time, Nikos, all in good time,' he continued, hiding his annoyance with Sylvie's attitude behind a mask of mild impatience. 'Yes, I am here for a few days' holiday, and Eleni may join us later.' He shrugged. 'As for how long I can stay——' He grimaced. 'That depends.'

Nikos pursed his lips. 'But you will let me show you how to build a castle, won't you? You won't spend all your time talking with Papa?'

'No.' Andreas was resigned. 'I will not spend all my time talking with your father.' He paused. 'But now I suggest you go and let Irene wash your face and hands, while I have a few words with—with Sylvie.'

'I can wash my own face and hands!' declared Nikos indignantly, but after a moment's hesitation, while he judged the seriousness of his uncle's expression, he shrugged his small shoulders and sauntered away.

Once they were alone, Andreas did not immediately break into speech, but instead moved away towards the low stone wall that separated the terrace from the beach, and stood staring broodingly into the distance. Sylvie, feeling the sun hot on her shoulders, moved into the shade until she could apply some of the sun-tan lotion she had been using, and realising she could not just walk away and leave him, seated herself in one of the low lounging chairs. The air was exquisite, warm and scented from the flowers, with just the faintest breeze to ruffle the fringe of the canopy above her.

'You had a letter from Margot,' Andreas said at last, without turning. 'Did she tell you when she expects to come back?'

Sylvie bent her head. 'No.'

Andreas turned. 'No?'

Sylvie looked up and met his dark gaze. 'The play's in rehearsal. She can't get away yet.' In all honesty, she didn't see how Margot was ever going to drag herself away, and her own reactions to that troubled her not a little.

Andreas's expression hardened. 'You mean this part she

was so desperate to take has not yet reached the performing stage?'

Sylvie plucked at the wooden arm of the chair. 'These things take time. A play needs money—backers. As far as I can gather, all the—the final details haven't yet been made.'

Andreas muttered a word that wasn't polite, then advanced across the flat stones towards her. Evidently the hot sun did not trouble him, and the brown skin of his shoulders gleamed with sweat. His hair too was moist around his ears and temples, but unlike her, he did not seek the shade.

'Exactly how long do you think this can go on?' he enquired, between thin lips. 'What precisely does Margot intend to do?'

Sylvie was obliged to tilt her head to look up at him, but the brilliance of the sun obscured her vision. 'I don't know,' she said helplessly, wishing they were not having this conversation. 'I think—well, Margot led me to believe that—that Nikos's nursemaid would be coming back.'

'Dora?'

'Yes, Dora.'

'But now you know she will not.'

'Why not?' Sylvie moistened her lips. 'Just because she's married it doesn't mean she can't have a job, too.'

'Later, perhaps,' agreed Andreas tautly. 'If her husband is short of money, and if he is agreeable. But not right away. I would imagine Dora will have her hands full in the not-too-distant future.'

Sylvie frowned. 'Oh?' His meaning was obvious. 'But——' she hesitated to say it, but it had to be said, '—you did say you intended to find a replacement.'

'I know what I said.' Andreas was curt. 'Unfortunately Leon does not agree with me. He does not want a replacement. He says he is quite happy with you.'

Sylvie could not deny the feeling of warmth this gave her, but even as she basked in its glow, the coldness of Andreas's eyes and the contemptuousness of his expression cast a chill.

'You don't approve?'

'You are damn right, I do not approve!' he snapped harshly, and Sylvie wished she had stood up while she still had the chance. Now, with him glowering down at her, she could not do so without putting herself too close to him for comfort, and instead she was forced to sit there and suffer his disapproval. 'Your behaviour appals me. Have you any idea what you are doing? What problems you are creating? Do you think I want Leon to recover his physical strength, if mentally you are crippling him?'

'That's not true!' Sylvie did get up now, levering herself out of the chair, her arm brushing his damp skin as she put its width between them. 'Leon and I are friends, that's all. Just friends! And—and brother-and sister-in-law, or had you forgotten?'

'And do you usually go around kissing the hands of your male relatives, in-laws or otherwise?' enquired Andreas scornfully, so that Sylvie's face suffused with colour.

'Leon—Leon's different!' she exclaimed hotly. 'I—I feel sympathy for him——'

'You pity him?'

'Perhaps.'

'But he does not pity you. Nor does he pity himself.'

'What are you saying?' Sylvie pressed her palms to her burning cheeks.

'I am saying that Leon is desperate for a relationship, *any* relationship—and you might be providing that relationship, whether you are aware of it or not.'

'You're wrong!' Sylvie turned away, breathing shallowly, gulping air into her lungs to dispel the feeling of faintness which had enveloped her.

'I hope so.' Andreas's cool voice was infuriatingly patronising, and she swung round on him angrily, only wishing to expunge a little of her own frustration.

'You'd know, of course,' she declared impulsively.
'Having, as you might say, sampled the goods yourself!
How do I know you're not jealous? Why should I believe
you, when you might have your own reasons for wanting
me to treat your brother differently?'

She had expected many reactions to her reckless outburst, but not the sound of his contemptuous laughter.
His dark eyes, surveying her with insolent appraisal,
mirrored the sardonic amusement on his face, and looking
at his sensual face and lean, muscular body, she wondered
at her own temerity in voicing such an outrageous proposition. His derision made her feel cheap, as well as childish,
and she wanted to lash out at him, but didn't know how.

'You could be right,' he said at last, mockingly.
'Perhaps I am—jealous, I mean. After all, you are a
most—how do they say it?—nubile young lady.'

Sylvie's jaw quivered, but she managed to conceal it,
and with a brief shrug of his shoulders he inclined his
head with ironic courtesy.

'Perhaps that is the answer,' he remarked consideringly,
almost as if he was speaking to himself, but Sylvie had
had enough.

'Go to hell!' she said, with bitter vehemence, and practically ran back into the villa to escape his expected response.

CHAPTER SEVEN

IT was an awful day. Sylvie divided her time between her room and the beach, unable to deny Nikos her company, but unwilling to lay herself open to further taunts from his uncle. Meals she managed to avoid, saying she wasn't hungry at lunchtime, and making the excuse that she had letters to write to eat dinner alone in her room. It was the first time she had done so since their arrival, but she hoped Leon's pleasure in his brother's company would compensate for her absence. After all, it could be argued that they might have things to say to one another that her presence would inhibit, and Thia Ariadne was much more a member of the family than she ever would be.

Yet it was Ariadne Petronides who eventually came looking for her, her gnarled fingers beating a tattoo on Sylvie's door as she sat by the french windows opening on to her balcony, watching the lights of a fishing boat anchored out in the bay. Unaware of the identity of her unexpected visitor, Sylvie opened the door tentatively, then stood back in relief when she saw who it was.

'Thia Ariadne!' she exclaimed. She had taken to using Leon and Nikos's name for her. 'What a surprise! Won't you come in?'

'I am not disturbing you?' Thia Ariadne's English was thick and heavily accented, but excellent for all that. 'Ah, I can see you have eaten little of your dinner. That was my anxiety.' Her dark eyes surveyed the girl intently. '*Etsi*, you are not feeling well, hmm?'

'I'm feeling fine, honestly.' Sylvie wrung her hands together behind her back as the old lady advanced into the room, closing the door behind her. 'I—er—I've been writing to my mother, that's all. And I wasn't particularly hungry.'

'As you were not hungry at lunchtime,' remarked Thia Ariadne, dryly. 'And yet until today you have had a very good appetite, *ohi*?'

'Perhaps it's the heat.' Sylvie forced a smile, pushing back her hair with a nervous hand, but the old lady was not deceived.

'Perhaps,' she agreed, giving her a moment's respite, and then added shrewdly: 'Or perhaps it is Andreas, hmm? I heard you arguing on the terrace this morning. What has he been saying to you? How has he upset you?'

Sylvie's lips parted helplessly. Was she always to be the one who was disconcerted? she thought fretfully. Why hadn't she considered Ariadne's normal practice of sitting, sewing, on her balcony, when she started raising her voice?

'I'm sorry,' she said now. 'Sorry if I disturbed you, I mean——'

'Oh, nonsense, child, you did not disturb me,' exclaimed Leon's aunt impatiently, seating herself in the chair Sylvie had previously occupied, and looking up at the girl with sharp, penetrating eyes. Although she must easily be seventy, her mind was as alert as it had ever been, and only her bony hands, plucking at the fichu about her shoulders, betrayed any trace of age or infirmity. 'But I know Andreas,' she continued firmly, bowing her head, 'and I know it is not usual for him to spend time here when there are so many other matters requiring his attention.'

'There are?'

Sylvie tried to divert the old lady in an effort to gain time, but she guessed Thia Ariadne would not have allowed herself to be sidetracked unless it was to her purpose to do so. 'Of course there are,' she exclaimed now, as if it was the most natural thing in the world. 'Andreas runs the company, but surely you knew that?' She looked up at the girl, and when Sylvie rather doubtfully shook her head, she went on: '*Kala*, he does. Since his father's health has given cause for concern, Andreas has taken the responsibility for the organisation on his shoulders, and with Leon incapacitated as he is, that is no small burden.'

'I suppose not.' Sylvie didn't quite see what this had to do with her, but Ariadne evidently thought she should know the truth.

'That is why I know there had to be a reason to bring him to Monastiros, not just his concern for his brother, which is unquestionable, but not enough.'

Sylvie moved her slim shoulders in an awkward gesture. 'You think his coming here has something to do with me?' The proposition was totally ludicrous, but that seemed to be what Thia Ariadne was saying.

'I think it has to do with you—and your sister,' declared the old lady firmly, and Sylvie experienced a sudden sense of deflation. 'I think Andreas may be blaming you for Margot's behaviour, and if this is so, then something must be said.' She squared her shoulders determinedly, before adding: 'I have never seen Nikos so animated, or so happy, and even Leon seems to be responding to your—how can I put it?—uninhibited youthfulness! Whatever Margot has done, however she has behaved, you cannot be held responsible for her actions, and if Andreas is using you to get at her, then he must be stopped.'

Sylvie expelled her breath on a shaky sigh. She realised it was the first time Thia Ariadne had shown herself aware of what was going on around her, but she should have remembered, she was Aristotle Petronides' sister. And if only it was that simple, she thought, moving into the shadows cast by the lamplight so that the old lady should not see her expression. If only all Andreas was concerned about was *Margot's* behaviour . . .

'Well?' The old lady was waiting for an answer, and Sylvie did not have one to give her.

'Andreas—Andreas doesn't blame me exactly,' she said at last, choosing her words with care. 'Our—our argument was about something else. Er—nothing important, nothing important at all.'

Thia Ariadne's greying brows descended and her scepticism was evident, but courtesy forbade her to say more. Pushing herself up out of the chair again, she smiled at Sylvie, and then, after a moment's hesitation, she said:

'Leon is looking much better, do you not agree? And he, too, urged me to find out if you were all right.' She paused. 'Then I can tell him you will join him for breakfast in the morning, *ne*? After your swim, of course.'

Sylvie licked her dry lips. 'All right.'

'*Kalo, kalo!*' Ariadne touched the girl's soft cheek with the back of her hand. '*Kalinichta*, Sylvie. Sleep well!'

Sylvie did not sleep well, she slept badly, for the first time since coming to the island, and she awakened with a feeling of resentment towards Andreas for disturbing her so. Why didn't he take his complaints to his brother? she thought indignantly, pushing her legs out of bed. It was Leon who was married, after all, not her, and if anyone was to blame, it should be him for creating the situation. Then she sighed. But that was ridiculous! How could Andreas approach Leon in his present condition—and besides, with a return of aggression, what was there to object to?

It was not a question she could answer. The night before she had gone over everything she and Leon had done together, and she could find little to reproach herself about. They were close, but that was only natural when two people shared the same house, the same meals, the same interests. She had never flirted with him, and to her knowledge he never overstepped the bounds of an affectionate elder brother. Oh, damn Andreas, she thought irritably, damn him for coming, damn him for putting doubts into her head, and damn him for spoiling an innocent relationship!

Tying on the scraps of a coffee-coloured bikini, she let herself out of her room and descended the stone staircase to the ground floor. The early morning sun was pouring through the cracks in the shutters, and the door creaked as she swung it back on its hinges. But beyond the shadows of the house the brilliance was blinding, and she raised her face to the heavens, closing her eyes and raising her arms above her head. She could understand the sun-worshippers of old, she thought, as she skipped lightly across the terrace and down the two steps to the sand. Who could believe such warmth and bounty could be given by anyone other than a god, and her spirits rose accordingly, uplifted by Apollo.

Dazzled as she was by the sun and her imagination, Sylvie was in the water and some distance out from the shore before she realised she was not alone. A few yards farther out, a dark head bobbed lazily on the waves, a lean, muscular body supported by the most indolent of strokes. It was Andreas, of course. It had to be. And Sylvie's frustration was complete as she turned back towards the beach. Not only had he come here disturbing her peace and her sleep, but now he was spoiling the one part of the day she considered completely her own, and angry tears sprang foolishly to her eyes.

'Hey!'

His attractive voice hailed her as she swam frantically for the shore, but Sylvie refused to acknowledge him. Let him have the water to himself, so long as he chose to stay here. She would enjoy it after he was gone, which surely couldn't be more than a few days from now.

'Sylvie!'

Impatience etched his tones, which were alarmingly

nearer now, and she could hear the sound of his movement through the water. He was evidently a much stronger swimmer than she was, and his unhurried strokes were rapidly gaining on her.

'Sylvie—wait!'

His words were uttered right behind her, and his hand reaching for her arm threw her into a ridiculous state of panic. She threshed about wildly, struggling to free herself, and his only course was to pull her against him, imprisoning her arms against her sides.

'*Theé mou*, stop fighting me!' he exclaimed, faint amusement in his eyes as they met the stormy amber of hers. 'What are you afraid of? I am not going to hurt you. But if you continue as you are doing, you may drown us both.'

'Then let me go!' she cried unsteadily, as the closeness of his body was rapidly banishing all other thoughts from her head. She could hardly believe it, but she could feel the muscled strength of his limbs against hers, and although her senses revoked the unwilling awareness, she was becoming convinced he was wearing nothing at all.

This realisation momentarily robbed her of all aggression, and her weakness made her yield momentarily against him ... before she could react he thrust her determinedly away from him.

Sylvie's cheeks were pink now, as much from embarrassment as indignation, and with an impatient movement of his head, Andreas put several feet between them. '*Entaxi*, so you are shocked,' he declared flatly. 'You were not meant to behave like a frightened colt, just because I wanted to talk to you.'

Sylvie swallowed hard, but she didn't do as her brain was frantically dictating and swim away from him. Somehow it was too late for that, and besides, she had his assurance now that all he wanted to do was talk to her.

'I—I don't see what we have to say to one another,' she said, keeping herself afloat without too much effort, and Andreas's dark eyes narrowed.

'No?' He paused. 'Not even when I tell you that Thia Ariadne spoke to me last evening, *after* she had been speaking to you?'

Sylvie held up her head, the wet coils of her hair floating about her. 'I can't imagine what your aunt could have told you that might make you think I would know what in the world you are talking about,' she retorted, rather obscurely. 'Thia Ariadne merely came to my room to enquire if I was feeling all right, that's all.'

'Is it?' Andreas's mouth twisted. 'And you deny telling her that I have been what is it you say?—bullying you, no?'

Sylvie guessed as much, but that didn't make it any easier to handle. 'If your aunt thinks you've been bullying me, then it's an impression she's gained, not me.' She drew a deep breath. 'I wouldn't dream of discussing you with her. I'm perfectly capable of handling my own affairs.'

'Oh, are you?' Andreas inclined his head sardonically. 'You mean by dodging the issue, I suppose.'

Sylvie's brows drew together. 'Dodging the issue?' she said confusedly.

'That is not how you would describe it?' he enquired, with mocking perception. 'What else would you call your determination to avoid me?'

Sylvie sniffed. She had guessed he would not be deceived by her paltry excuses, but she had hoped he would be too polite to confront her with them. She should have known better.

'You flatter yourself,' she said now, refusing to admit anything to him. 'It was true. I wasn't hungry at lunchtime, and in the evening I had some letters to write.'

'Obviously very important letters,' he mocked, glancing up at the sun as he slicked back his hair with long wet fingers.

'Obviously,' she agreed, stiffening as he swam round her in a wide circle, before returning to the attack.

'You were afraid to show your face,' he charged her coolly. 'You were afraid I might be shown to be right.' He hesitated. 'It may interest you to know that your absence did not improve my brother's appetite either.'

Sylvie heaved a sigh. 'Is that all you have to say to me, Mr Petronides?' she exclaimed. 'Because if you don't mind, I'd like to go and get dressed before breakfast.'

'What about your swim?' asked Andreas annoyingly. 'I understood from Leon that you swim every morning.'

'And no doubt you set out to waylay me!' she retorted.

Andreas's thin lips curved. 'You might say that.'

Sylvie's indignation rose. 'You mean you did!'

'Why not?'

'You know why not!' She was incensed.

'Oh——' He grimaced. 'Because I am not wearing any shorts.' His expression became mocking. 'I regret, I did not bring any with me.'

'Then—then you should have—have worn something else. A pair of—of Leon's, perhaps.'

'I do not wear my brother's clothes,' replied Andreas mildly. 'And I did not know you were so prudish, Sylvie. You, who declares herself so capable of taking care of herself.'

'You—you wouldn't have done this if—if I'd been a Greek girl!' exclaimed Sylvie resentfully. 'Oh, you—you're detestable!' and with a sudden turn she swam strongly back to the shore.

She was several yards up the beach when he caught her, grasping her arms from behind and pulling her back against him. 'I do not intend that you shall walk away from me again,' he declared, his breath warm against her ear, and without giving her time to protest, he twisted her round in his arms and imprisoned her mouth beneath his.

His kiss was hard and hungry, demanding a response and gaining it from her unprepared lips, and the sensuality of their embrace was heightened every minute she was pressed against him. But her outrage at his insistence was weakened by her discovery that he had taken the time to wrap a towel around his waist.

She wanted to tell him to let her go, but her lips parted involuntarily, and his tongue against her sensitized skin ignited her emotions. Almost convulsively, her arms arched upward, around his neck, gripping the hair on his nape and pulling him closer. The thin cotton of her bikini was hardly a barrier to the thrusting fullness of her breasts, and the hair on his stomach was disturbingly rough and male against her midriff.

'This was not my intention,' he muttered huskily, when he released her lips long enough to gather drops of moisture from the curve of her cheek with his tongue. 'But you are so—so desirable, you make me do things I know I will regret!'

Sylvie's senses were spinning, the dazzling brilliance of the sun making her close her eyes so that all she could think about and feel was Andreas's closeness, his lovemaking, his devastating assault on her emotions. Her lashes fanned like a dark shadow on her cheeks, her lips were parted, inviting his invasion, and her sun-kissed limbs curved into his, seeking intimacy. All sense of time and place had left her, and it was Andreas who had to push her away at last, holding her from him with hands that bit into her flesh.

'Sylvie!' he muttered, as she swayed dizzily before him. 'Sylvie, what are you trying to do to me?' And as her eyes jerked open: 'For God's sake, you cannot be that naïve!'

Sylvie gazed at him half uncomprehendingly for a moment, and then, realising the ignominy of her position, freed herself. Pushing back the dripping length of her hair, she endeavoured to recover a sense of proportion, desperately anxious that Andreas should not become aware of how shaken she was.

Andreas, for his part, was turning away, and now she saw the denim shorts lying on the sand. Their existence suddenly infuriated her, reminding her as they did of his deliberate attempt to humiliate her, and the words rushed out of her as he bent to pick them up.

'I wonder what Leon or your aunt would say if they knew what you had done!' she exclaimed contemptuously. 'I wonder how Thia Ariadne would react if I told her you had gone swimming in the nude. Particularly, when you knew—you *expected*—me to join you!'

Andreas paused, regarding her between narrowed lids. 'Do you really think I care what Leon or Ariadne think?' he demanded harshly. 'I am not a child, Sylvie. I live my own life. And how I choose to treat provocative little girls like you is my own business, no one—and I mean no one—has the right to stop me.'

Sylvie caught her breath. 'I don't believe you.'

He bowed his head. 'That is your prerogative, of course.' His lips curled. 'But I should tell you, if you think your threats will trap me into marriage, as your sister trapped my brother, then you are wasting your time.'

Sylvie gasped. 'Marriage? Do you think I would marry you?' She shook her head disbelievingly.

Andreas shrugged. 'You mean I can have you without marriage?'

'No!' Sylvie's face was crimson. 'How—how dare you——'

Andreas's dark eyes were mocking. 'My dear child, I could have taken you just now, a few moments ago, had I had a mind to provide the seabirds with such a spectacle——'

'No——'

'—and if you say you do not want marriage,' he continued inexorably, 'then I can only assume you will settle for something else.'

'You—bastard!'

Andreas's mouth hardened. 'That is not the language of a young lady. And I am beginning to think you are more like Margot than I suspected.'

'Why?' Sylvie felt suddenly hot and miserable. In any argument with him, she came out the loser, and quite unexpectedly she felt near to tears.

'Why?' Andreas seemed taken aback by her question, and for a moment he regarded her with steady appraisal. Then, as if aware of her inner turmoil, he turned away. 'Go and get dressed, Sylvie,' he advised her tautly. 'I suggest we try and forget this—this conversation ever took place. Perhaps I have been rather—cruel. Perhaps you make me that way. In any event, this situation must not be repeated, and it is as well that Eleni is joining us tomorrow. Perhaps she will help you to keep things in perspective.'

Leon was at the breakfast table when Sylvie emerged from the villa after taking a shower. As on the previous day, he was wearing shorts and leather sandals, and his thin face broke into a warm smile when she seated herself beside him.

'Where were you yesterday?' he exclaimed, after she had asked after his health, and been assured that he felt stronger every day. 'I missed you. Do not let Andreas frighten you away. I know you feel the outsider here, but believe me when I say I would rather talk to you than practically anyone else.'

Sylvie forced a smile, but his words were unpleasantly familiar after what his brother had said, and she hated Andreas anew for making her so absurdly sensitive. In consequence, her response was warmer than it might have been otherwise, and Leon was holding one of her hands between both of his when Andreas came out of the villa.

He, too, had bathed and changed, drops of moisture still sparkling on the smooth darkness of his hair. He was wearing the jeans he had worn to come in, and a navy cotton vest, and his dominant vitality was in direct contrast to his brother's paler image. His eyes flicked carelessly over Sylvie, assessing her simple poplin suit and dismissing it. If he observed their closeness he made no mention of the fact, but merely flung himself in the chair opposite and greeted his brother with genuine enthusiasm.

Immediately Sylvie felt discomfited, whether he intended it or otherwise. The poplin shorts and halter top, which in her bedroom had looked bright and attractive, now felt skimpy and childish, and she wished she had not plaited her hair, which made her look more like a schoolgirl.

'I thought I might drive into the village this morning, and take the ferry over to Piso,' Andreas remarked, after Irene had brought him some fresh rolls and coffee. 'It is some time since I have seen Riva, and I promised him I would call the next time I came to Monastiros.' He paused, then said, deliberately, Sylvie felt: 'I thought I might take Nikos with me.' His eyes met hers for an instant and then moved on. 'To give—Sylvie—a break, hmm?' His lips twisted with faint maliciousness. 'What do you think, Leon?'

Leon hesitated, looking first at his brother, then at Sylvie, and finally back to his brother again. 'I think perhaps you should take Sylvie,' he said at last, and as she started to protest, he added: 'It is true. She has not had a rest from the boy since our arrival, and I think——'

'I don't need a rest!' Sylvie interrupted him determinedly. 'Honestly, Leon, Nikos and I——'

'But you have seen nothing of the islands yet, have you,

little one?' Leon persisted gently. 'Listen to me——' This, as her lips parted in denial. 'You will enjoy yourself with Andreas. He is not a poor creature like me——'

'Leon!' Sylvie gazed helplessly at him. 'Leon, Andreas didn't ask me!' She was flushed and embarrassed again, as well as angry. 'Please——'

'Naturally, if Sylvie would like to accompany me, I should be delighted to escort her,' inserted Andreas at this point, his tone cool and infuriatingly controlled. 'I could take them both——'

Like children together, thought Sylvie frustratedly, but Leon did not see it that way.

'Nikos will stay here,' he averred firmly. 'We will enjoy having a day together. Surely you would not deprive me of both my companions at one time?' he added lightly.

Sylvie sighed. 'Leon——'

'Go, little one. Go and enjoy yourself. This is your holiday—remember that.'

Sylvie's eyes were stormy when she looked at Andreas, and his almost imperceptible shrug did not help. It was as if he was denying all responsibility for what had taken place, and although she did not want to accept it, she had to concede he was not to blame.

Oh, Leon, she thought helplessly, turning her eyes on the man watching her with such tender compassion. Why had he to interfere? If only he had just let Andreas go. She didn't want to spend a whole day in his company. She didn't even *like* him. And it was certain sure that he did not want to spend the day with her!

CHAPTER EIGHT

THE little caique that served as a ferryboat between the islands was not crowded, but there was much noise and laughter and goodnatured argument between its passengers, and the clucking of hens from a crate stowed on the engine housing added their own peculiar protest to the mêlée. The caique was an ungainly-looking vessel, that rocked rather alarmingly when Sylvie stepped aboard, but once under way it rode the gentle waves smoothly, with only the occasional swell to disturb a nervous stomach.

Sylvie seated herself at the far end of the wooden planking that ran along the side of the vessel, deliberately turning her back on Andreas as she draped one honey-brown arm over the rail. If she had to accompany him, then so be it, but she was not going to allow herself to be accused of engineering this particular outing. It was obvious he did not want to take her, and certainly she had no desire to go. But Leon would have become suspicious of her motives if she had continued to argue against it, and Andreas's sardonic expression had revealed what he thought of her protests.

She had taken the time to change, however, discarding the halter top and shorts in favour of a bikini and a matching wrap-around skirt. The outfit had been Margot's, many moons ago, but styles had changed and her sister had offered it to her, and the twelve-year-old Sylvie, as she then was, had jumped at the chance of an expensive beach suit. Now she suspected the skirt was a little short for fashionable wear, and its beaded piping was definitely dated, but the colour, a kind of dusty pink edged with white, suited her, and she felt more at ease with her thighs safely covered.

The caique had a canvas canopy rigged haphazardly across the central area, and the shadow it cast meant Sylvie's shoulders would be protected from the increasing glare of the sun. She had chosen the sheltered side deliberately, so that she wouldn't feel uncomfortable, but she sighed in exasperation when the caique pulled away from the harbour, swinging round so that she was on the unprotected side after all.

'I could have told you, if you had asked,' remarked Andreas behind her, and she swung round mutinously, fixing him with an angry glare.

'But of course you had to be asked, didn't you?' she snapped, infuriated by his cool indifference to the heat, and he inclined his head politely as she fumed over her mistake.

'Why do you not go and sit over there?' he enquired, gesturing lazily across the boat to where two elderly Greek women were gossiping together, oblivious to the heat. There was room for one, wedged between them and some crates, and after a moment's hesitation Sylvie nodded.

'Why not?' she declared, getting up. 'Their company can't be any more objectionable than yours!' and picking her way across a pile of ropes, she did as he suggested.

As she got nearer the women, however, the smell of fish became unmistakable, and she realised suddenly what was in the crates. If she seated herself beside them, she would soon smell as strongly as they did, and her lips twitched in frustration as she stumbled ignominiously back to her previous position.

Andreas looked up in mild amusement as she took her seat beside him, and then glanced sideways at her after she had settled herself to her satisfaction. 'No luck?' he asked innocently, arching his dark brows, and she had to steel herself furiously to suppress the desire to strike him.

'You knew!' she accused him in a low voice. 'You knew what was in those crates!'

Andreas shrugged. 'I see.' He paused. 'Do I take it then that my company is preferable to raw fish?' he queried with wry humour, and Sylvie couldn't prevent the smile that suddenly parted her compressed lips. Andreas was watching her, his dark face mirroring her expression, and with a sigh of impatience she lay back against the rail and moved her head from side to side in a gesture of defeat.

'Why did you agree to bring me?' she exclaimed. 'Why didn't you protest? You know you didn't want me to come, so why didn't you tell Leon so?'

Andreas moved his shoulders indolently. 'Did I say I did not want you to come?' he exclaimed, resting his elbows on the rail behind him, and she sobered as she remembered exactly what he had said earlier.

'You offered to take Nikos,' she declared carefully. She turned her head to look at him. 'Not me.'

Andreas contemplated the view before speaking again. Miles and miles of glistening water stretched to the horizon, dazzling in its brilliance. 'Perhaps I guessed what Leon would say,' he remarked at last. 'My brother is nothing if not honourable.'

Sylvie digested this. 'But why?' she asked helplessly. 'After what you said——'

'Let us forget what I said, for today at least,' Andreas suggested flatly. 'Do as Leon said. Enjoy the day for what it brings.'

It was about eleven o'clock when the caique docked at the jetty on the small island of Piso. Andreas sprang up on to the stone quay and held out his hand to Sylvie. After a moment's hesitation she took it, allowing him to haul her up beside him, flushing when for a brief moment his steadying hand was hard upon her waist.

Piso was very like Monastiros, a cluster of whitewashed cottages clustered about the harbour, with the bare, rocky hillside rising behind. A dusty track, it was hardly a road, led up from the harbour, and silhouetted against the skyline was the simple austerity of a small monastery.

Andreas did not take this track, however, but set off along the coastal strip, soon leaving the village behind, and following a path over a rocky promontory and down through orange groves, cultivated, he explained, for the tourist trade on one of the larger islands.

'Nothing grows naturally here, except perhaps the lizards,' he amended, as a pale yellow body slithered hastily between the rocks, and Sylvie suppressed the slight shiver its darting beady eyes had promoted.

She wondered where they were going, and how far it was. Already she was soaked with sweat, the hair that had escaped from its braiding, clinging in moist tendrils to her forehead and the nape of her neck. She was afraid her face was red and blotchy with the heat, and that she looked as exhausted as she felt, and she wished they could rest a while and recover in the shade of some cool awning.

'That is our destination—see!'

Andreas had halted, waiting for her to catch up with him, and as she did so, panting in her efforts to regain her breath, she looked down on a most desirable scene. Below them was a small cove, and set slightly above it was a square stone house. The house was not large, but it was evidently inhabited, and as they approached down the stony slope, Sylvie could see goats grazing nearby and chickens pecking in the earth at the back.

'This—this is your friend—Riva's house?' she ventured breathlessly, struggling to retain her footing, and Andreas nodded before jumping down the last few feet and turning to bid her to do the same. Sylvie jumped, mainly because she couldn't wait to get indoors out of the glare of the sun, but when Andreas caught her and held her momentarily against his chest, that proposition suddenly seemed less important. But remembering what he had said, she pushed him away, and with a wry inclination of his head Andreas accepted her dismissal and led the way round the building to the shaded verandah.

A man of perhaps forty was seated on the verandah, his feet stretched out in front of him, arms folded, eyes closed. He was wearing nothing but a disreputable pair of baggy pants and a wide-brimmed hat tipped over his forehead. There was a bottle of wine on the table nearby, with a half empty glass standing beside it. But what attracted Sylvie's attention were the sketches strewn carelessly all over the table and the floor, and the curled-up balls of paper that betrayed efforts attempted and discarded. And they were brilliant sketches, too, she realised wonderingly, vivid likenesses of a face she had seen over and over since her arrival in Greece. It was the face of an old woman, gnarled and weatherbeaten, yet possessing a wealth of character that made her seem almost real.

Andreas grimaced at the mess, then unsympathetically jolted the man's legs from their relaxed position. '*Ti ine afto*, Angelos,' he chided sardonically. '*Ehete tipota na kano?*'

'*Ti?*' The man started up in surprise, blinking uncomprehendingly at Sylvie. Then, swinging his head round, he saw Andreas, and his look of blank insensibility changed to one of warm indulgence. '*Oriste*, Andreas! *Embros! Embros! Ti kanete?*'

'*Kala, kala . . .*' Andreas responded to the other man's embrace with goodnatured enthusiasm, submitting to his repeated pats on the back with a lazily mocking smile. Then, turning to Sylvie, he said: 'Angelos, I would like to introduce you to my sister-in-law Sylvie. You remember— Margot's sister? She has joined us for a visit, but she does not speak our language.'

'*Ohi?*' Angelos surveyed Sylvie with a disturbingly intent gaze. 'I am most pleased to meet you, *thespinis*. Welcome to my humble abode.'

'How do you do?' Sylvie shook hands politely, and finding Andreas's eyes upon her too, was briefly glad of her hot face to hide her feelings of awkwardness and embarrassment. 'I—er—are these your sketches?' She moistened her lips when he did not immediately reply. 'They're very good.'

'Thank you. I am glad you like my work.' Angelos Riva bowed his head deferentially. On his feet, he was still shorter than Andreas, but sturdier, stockier, with the curly dark hair Sylvie was more used to seeing. He had a moustache, too, that curled down to his jawline, giving him a somewhat piratical appearance, but his smile was self-confident as well as infectious, and she doubted he needed her immature approval.

'Angelos's work is not unknown in Greece—as well as in a few other places,' remarked Andreas dryly, and Sylvie, intercepting the glance he exchanged with the other man, felt even worse.

'What my friend is trying to say is that I paint a little,' inserted Angelos, taking pity on her. He put out his hand suddenly, startling her by tilting her face into the light. 'Perhaps I will paint you, *thespinis*. The face is inexperienced, but the bone structure is good.'

Sylvie pulled her chin away, helpless at the mercy of two such sophisticated men, and Angelos laughed, and made a gesture of apology, saying something to Andreas in their own language that made the younger man regard her with mocking interrogation.

'*Etsi,*' said Angelos at last, indicating that Sylvie should sit down, and offering Andreas some of the wine. 'What brings you to Piso? Do you have a mind to teach your little sister the delights of diving off the headland?'

Sylvie's brows arched, but she sank down thankfully into the chair that was offered as Andreas said: 'She's not my little sister, Angelos. And perhaps I will take her out in the bay. But diving—not today, I think. The face mask is enough.'

Angelos nodded, and then turned to Sylvie again, saying gently: 'You must be thirsty, *thespinis*. Some Coke, perhaps? Or some fruit cordial? Even in this remote place, I manage to chill my ice-box, and I can even offer you ice-cream, if that would please you.'

Sylvie was suddenly angered by the patronising tone of his voice. How old did he think she was, for God's sake? Surely she didn't look like a schoolgirl?

'I am eighteen, you know,' she declared stiffly. 'I do drink wine, and alcohol occasionally.' She pursed her lips. 'But Coke would be very nice.'

Angelos grinned. 'My apologies, *thespinis*. I thought— well, no matter. Coke it shall be. One moment, please.'

When they were alone, Sylvie looked up at Andreas half accusingly. 'How old do I look?' she demanded irritably. 'Fifteen? Sixteen?'

'With your hair like that—perhaps,' he commented indifferently, moving to the low wall of the verandah and resting his hips upon it. 'That's what makes you so provocative, did you not know? The mind of a child, and the body of a woman.'

Sylvie was still digesting this when Angelos returned, carrying some glasses and two bottles of Coke. 'My friend drinks only fruit juice when he goes diving in the bay,' he said, half mocking, half apologetic, as he handed the second Coke to Andreas. 'Forgive me if you thought I was being rude earlier. I did not expect Andreas's little sister to prefer a stronger beverage.'

'I have told you, Angelos, she is not my sister,' Andreas averred dryly, refusing a glass and drinking from the bottle. 'And she does not prefer a stronger beverage. She was only fooling.'

'Really?' Angelos looked sceptical, but Sylvie refused to be baited further, and putting down her glass, she rose from her seat and stepped down on to the beach below the verandah. The sand was warm, even through her sandals, and kicking them off, she padded to the water's edge.

The water curling round her toes was deliciously soft, and after only a moment's hesitation she dropped her skirt and ran into the waves. It wasn't cold, but it was refreshing, and all the stickiness of the journey, and her embarrassment at their hands, was washed away in the space of a few moments. She hardly had to use her arms at all. The water was so buoyant she floated effortlessly, and it was some minutes later that she remembered where she was, and how impolitely her behaviour could be construed.

The splash of someone nearby caused her to open her eyes fully, and allowing her legs to sink, she looked about her rather apprehensively. She had not forgotten earlier this morning, and Andreas's apparent indifference to her modesty, and the sight of his dark head only a few feet away caused her no minor upheaval.

He was swimming towards her, and she put out her hand warningly, as if to hold him off. 'What do you think you're doing?' she cried, as he got progressively nearer, and his lips parted in a knowing grin as he interpreted her reactions.

'I thought—if you have recovered from your outrage— that we might do a little snorkelling,' he remarked, and as her eyes adjusted themselves once more to the clarity of the light, Sylvie realised his body looked black below the level of the water. He was wearing a rubber suit, and she was too relieved to protest when he came up beside her.

'Do—do I have to wear something like that?' she asked doubtfully, not at all confident of her appearance in something so revealing, but Andreas shook his head.

'This is for scuba-diving,' he explained patiently, bidding her follow him back to the shore. 'Come on, I think you will like this. Have you ever tried it before?'

Sylvie hadn't, but in no time at all she had mastered the art of breathing through the long tube that was attached to a face mask. It made her eyes smart, the first time she endeavoured to dive underwater, however, and her throat felt sore after prolonged efforts to breathe through her mouth. But gradually she became more confident, swimming some distance out from the shore, the tube safely above water, her masked face only inches below. It was a revelation. There was so much to see. The floor of the ocean was not thickly foliaged as she had seen in films of explorations that had taken place in more southerly waters, but the varieties of fish and the different kinds of rock formation were endless, and her indignation with Andreas gave way to a genuine gratitude for his having given her this experience.

'I really do appreciate it,' she exclaimed, as she walked up out of the water with him, after he had accompanied her out to the headland and back. She pulled off the mask and wiped the moisture from her face. 'It was marvellous!'

Andreas's smile was deprecating. 'It was worth the journey?'

'Oh, yes.' Sylvie looked up at him frankly. 'Thank you.'

Andreas's dark eyes flickered over her scantily-clad body, then he turned abruptly away, hoisting the oxygen tanks he had left on the beach earlier for his own particular recreation. 'Tell Angelos I will be back in thirty minutes,' he said, pulling up the strap between his legs and securing it firmly, and Sylvie nodded, her lower lip caught between her teeth as he walked back into the water and disappeared from her sight.

The scraps of her swimsuit would soon dry in the hot

sun, and the briefs barely dampened her skirt as she wrapped it about her. Angelos was not on the verandah when she climbed the steps, however, and she went tentatively to the door of the building and called his name.

He appeared almost at once, from a room at the back of the house, and as Sylvie's nose reacted to the delicious aroma he brought with him, Angelos gestured that she should come in. She followed him into a stone-flagged kitchen and saw that he was in the process of preparing lunch. A delicious concoction of rice and prawns in a creamy sauce was simmering on the stove, and on the scrubbed wooden table in front of her there was cheese, and fresh bread, and a mouthwatering bunch of grapes.

'Help yourself, if you are hungry,' Angelos advised, observing her longing look at the food. 'We do not stand on ceremony here. When we are thirsty we drink, and when we are hungry we eat. Is that not a more civilised philosophy than setting times for meals, hmm?'

Sylvie smiled. 'I suppose so.'

'So—where is Andreas?'

'Oh——' Sylvie paused in the process of cutting herself a piece of cheese. 'He's gone scuba-diving. He said to tell you he would be back in half an hour.'

'Ah,' Angelos nodded. 'Good. That gives the pilaff more time to cook. If I had known you were coming, I could have killed a chicken, but as it is, the prawns will have to do.'

'They smell delicious,' said Sylvie honestly. 'Do you live here alone, Mr Riva?'

'Angelos,' he said firmly. 'Call me Angelos.' His eyes twinkled. 'I am not so old that a young lady needs to treat me deferentially.'

Sylvie acknowledged the teasing reference to her earlier reproval, but somehow, without Andreas's knowing eyes upon her, she felt more relaxed. 'So—Angelos,' she said obediently. 'Is this your home?'

'It is my home on Piso,' he agreed, stirring the contents of the saucepan, and Sylvie sighed.

'That isn't quite an answer, is it?' she commented. 'Does that mean you have a home somewhere else?'

Angelos glanced at her. 'Perhaps.'

Sylvie grimaced, and seated herself on the wooden bench, set at one side of the table. 'I take it you're really a very successful portrait painter.'

'I have had some luck,' he conceded, turning to help himself to more wine, raising his glass towards her with a rueful smile. 'It is to Andreas I owe my good fortune. Without his support—and his faith—I should never have progressed beyond sketching likenesses for the tourists at a few drachs a time.'

'You—you've known Andreas a long time?' Sylvie asked.

'More than twenty years,' he agreed, sighing reminiscently. 'I used to work for his father, you understand? When Andreas was still at school. I was the chauffeur, and in my spare time . . .'

' . . . you sketched likenesses for the tourists?'

Angelos nodded. '*Ehete thikeo*. You are right. So many years ago.'

Sylvie munched thoughtfully on the cheese. Then, choosing her words carefully, she said: 'So you probably know the girl he—he was going to marry.'

'Eleni?' Angelos smiled. 'Yes, I know Eleni. Andreas was very fond of her.'

'So why didn't he marry her?'

The question was out before Sylvie could prevent it, but to her relief, Angelos did not seem to find it presumptuous. 'I do not think Andreas was in love with Eleni, not then,' he said slowly. 'He was young. He was not long out of the university. He did not want to be—what would you say?—tied down, *ohi*?'

Sylvie bent her head. 'And Eleni married someone else.'

'Giorgios Frederiks, *ne*. A man more than twice her age, but with the fortune she so desperately craved.'

Sylvie looked up at him, but Angelos was already moving away, attending to the pan on the small gas stove. It was obvious he felt he had said enough, maybe too much. Either way, he was indicating that that particular part of their conversation was over.

By the time Andreas returned, entering the kitchen like some avenging sea-god, water dripping heedlessly all over the flagged floor, Sylvie and Angelos had progressed beyond his work to their individual likes and dislikes in the world of art and literature. The painter looked quite sorry when the other man's arrival interrupted their discussion, and Andreas commented rather dryly that he obviously hadn't been missed.

'We have just been sharing our opinions of neo-Impressionism,' declared Angelos cheerfully, pouring himself more wine. 'Your little sister is a radical, Andreas, my friend. She actually likes the work of Angelos Meya.'

Sylvie could not understand Andreas's suddenly mocking smile, but his next words helped to clarify the situation. 'And does she know who Angelos Meya is?' he inquired, pausing in the doorway, on his way to change.

Sylvie stared at him, then at Angelos, and then back to Andreas again. 'Angelos Meya!' she exclaimed. '*Angelos!* You mean—you——' She turned back to the other man, and he chuckled.

'I confess I am he,' he agreed, with a careless shrug of his shoulders. 'But I hope that will not prevent you from enjoying my prawn pilaff. I assure you, my talents are not limited to the easel.'

It was late when they left Angelos to walk back to the

harbour to catch the evening ferry. Already the crickets were performing their nightly ritual, and the incessant scraping of their legs was like some tuneless concerto for violin.

'Did you enjoy yourself?' asked Andreas quietly, as they lounged on the harbour wall, watching the lights of the ferry as it approached across the bay, and Sylvie glanced at him ruefully.

'You know I did. He's a fascinating man. And he's done so much in his life.' She sighed. 'Travelling to all those exotic places! Hawaii, Fiji—South America!' She shook her head. 'You must feel very pleased with yourself.'

'With myself,' Andreas made a sound of disbelief.

'Yes.' Sylvie frowned. 'You recognised his talent. You helped him to achieve his ambition——'

'With or without my help, Angelos would have made it,' retorted Andreas flatly. 'He owes me no credit for anything.'

'That's not what he thinks,' declared Sylvie, pursing her lips. 'And nor do I. I—I think he has a lot to thank you for.'

'Really?' Andreas's brows arched cynically. 'Do I detect a trace of approval in your voice for once?'

Sylvie's lips twitched. 'Don't spoil it. I've enjoyed my day, and I'm grateful.'

'How grateful?' murmured Andreas narrowly, and she bent her head rather quickly, so that he should not see her face.

The arrival of the caique prevented any further discussion right then, but once on board their intimacy was pronounced by the absence of many other passengers, the melodic strains of *bouzouki* music drifting from the pilot's radio, and the fading light that was a benediction for lovers.

'So—tell me,' he said, leaning his back against the rail beside her, 'what else did you enjoy about your day?'

'Oh—I enjoyed Angelos's pilaff, and swimming this afternoon. And sunbathing. And your company, of course.'

'Why "of course"? So far, my company has not seemed to your taste?'

'Oh, that was because——'

She broke off abruptly, but Andreas prompted her, adding softly: 'Go on, say it. Tell me what you think.'

Sylvie hesitated. 'No, it's not important. Not right now anyway.' She paused. 'Did you enjoy today?'

Andreas's mouth twisted. 'How could I not? With such a charming companion!'

'You're teasing me!' Sylvie pursed her lips. 'Did you mind wearing Angelos's swimming trunks?'

'Was there an alternative?'

She tilted her head away from him. 'No. Besides, they suited you. You have nice legs.'

Andreas shook his head. 'Did no one ever tell you, you do not make comments like that?'

'Why not?' Sylvie was beginning to enjoy this. 'It's the truth. You do have nice legs. They're not all white and knobbly, like some boys' I've seen.'

'I am not a boy, Sylvie,' Andreas averred, with sudden emphasis. 'I am almost forty! Almost middle-aged! You, on the other hand, are just an adolescent.'

'Thirty-four is not middle-aged!' retorted Sylvie at once, and his eyes narrowed.

'How do you know how old I am? Who told you? Angelos?'

'As a matter of fact it was Marina,' admitted Sylvie reluctantly. 'I asked her, and she told me.'

'I see.' Andreas rested his elbows on the rail behind him. 'That must have amused her.'

'No!' Sylvie was indignant. 'Marina's not like that.'

'You like Marina?'

'Yes.'

'Perhaps she should have come with you to Monastiros, instead of Thia Ariadne,' he observed flatly.

'Why?' Sylvie was puzzled.

'Thia Ariadne is old. Perhaps her eyesight is not as good as it used to be.'

Sylvie sighed disappointedly. 'You're talking about Leon and me again, aren't you? You promised you'd forget that for today, at least.'

'Do you not think it is a safer topic?' he enquired, with sudden impatience, and Sylvie's skin prickled as she considered this disclosure.

'How—how long are you staying?' she asked impulsively. 'Over the weekend?'

Andreas moved his broad shoulders indifferently. 'I am not sure,' he replied, his voice perceptibly cooler suddenly. 'Eleni arrives tomorrow. If she wants to stay, we will stay.'

Sylvie absorbed this reluctantly, and when he half turned away to watch for the lights of Monastiros, she leaned disconsolately on the rail. Everything had gone unexpectedly flat, and she realised with a pang that by asking how long he was staying she had reminded him of the other girl's visit. What did he really feel about Eleni Frederiks? Was he going to marry her, as his family seemed to expect? And what was it to do with her, when he had made it plain that he regarded her as little more than a diverting teenager?

CHAPTER NINE

THE next morning followed the pattern of all Sylvie's mornings since she had come to Monastiros. She swam before breakfast, undisturbed by any unwelcome intruders, and then, after having breakfast with Leon and Nikos, she took the small boy down to the beach. Andreas had not put in an appearance, and she assumed he must be making the most of his rest before Eleni arrived and he was obliged to accommodate her, and therefore she was surprised just before lunch when a dinghy sailed into the cove with Andreas at the helm.

Nikos was very excited, running across the sand to where his uncle was climbing out of the beached dinghy, and gesticulating furiously that he wanted to be taken for a ride. Sylvie, after a moment's hesitation, followed the boy, brushing sand from her hot limbs, and pushing back the two bunches of hair she had fastened with elastic bands above her ears.

'Thios Andreas is going to take me out in the boat,' exclaimed Nikos, as she drew near them, and Sylvie nodded her unwilling approval when his uncle endorsed the statement.

'Why do you not join us?' he invited, but the dark eyes were guarded, and remembering his coolness the night before, Sylvie shook her head.

'I'm too hot,' she averred, putting her palm on the crown of her head. 'You go, Nikos. I will see you at lunch. Be careful!'

Nikos nodded, but he was already scrambling into the boat, and Sylvie guessed he was not paying attention.

'He will be all right. I will take care of him,' declared Andreas quietly, as she was about to turn away. 'There are life-jackets in the locker and I will see he wears one. You need not worry on his account.'

'Good.' Sylvie's tone was clipped. 'See you later, then.'

'See you later,' agreed Andreas shortly, and she watched as he pushed the dinghy into deeper water before swinging himself on board. He was wearing the denim shorts he had worn on his first morning at the villa, and as she walked up the beach again, trudging her feet through the sand, she reflected rather irritably that he was one of the few men she had seen who looked as good with his clothes off as with them on. He did have nice legs, she thought, scuffing her toes, but the rest of him was equally attractive. It wasn't fair, she decided, sniffing a little resentfully. She had never met anyone quite like him before. Yet he blamed her for provoking him, when every movement he made aroused feelings inside her that there seemed no way to assuage.

Leon was resting when she got back to the villa, so she took a cold shower and felt infinitely better after it. She dressed in a cotton vest that tied on the shoulder and a brushed denim skirt, spurning a swimsuit in favour of a more conventional outfit. She brushed out her hair, securing it with a leather thong at her nape, and felt reasonably ready to face the opposition when Eleni chose to put in an appearance. She wondered how the other girl intended to get here. Would she use the ferry, or had she her own means of transport? Whatever, Sylvie guessed she would arrive in the afternoon, and her spirits drooped in anticipation of her intervention.

Lunch was served late, due to the fact that Andreas and Nikos did not arrive back until half past one. The little boy came bounding up on to the terrace, where his father and Sylvie were sitting together sharing a jug of iced cordial, and couldn't wait to tell them how exciting his trip had been. Leon had casually disclosed that the dinghy belonged to Andreas, and that he kept it berthed down at the harbour, and Sylvie reflected disconsolately that no doubt he had really rescued it from its mooring for Eleni's benefit.

Andreas followed his nephew on to the terrace, flinging himself into a chair by the table and grinning at his brother with easy tolerance. '*Theos*, it is hot!' he exclaimed, rubbing the back of his hand across his forehead. And as Irene appeared he bade her fetch him a lager, before serving the meal she had delayed for his benefit.

'I gather you have had a good morning, *adhelfe*,' Leon remarked smilingly, as his son moved away to pour himself some cordial, gulping it thirstily. 'Nikos has enjoyed himself, that is certain, and I appreciate your concern for him, and the time that you have given him.'

Andreas shrugged, his gaze moving briefly to Sylvie as she wiped Nikos's sticky mouth with a tissue. 'It was a pleasure,' he assured Leon shortly, giving Irene a grateful nod as she brought his lager. 'I guessed he had never sailed before, and the wind was not too strong.'

'No.' Leon looked skyward, a frown puckering his forehead as he observed its brassy glare. 'Yet I think we may have a storm later. There is a certain heaviness to the air.'

'Perhaps.' Andreas studied the can of lager in his hands with brooding concentration. 'I doubt you are right. The sea is too calm.'

Leon shrugged. 'Oh, well . . .' He looked at Sylvie. 'Shall we eat now? I feel quite hungry. How about you?'

Sylvie forced a smile. 'I suppose I am a little hungry,' she conceded, though in all honesty she had practically no appetite at all.

The meal was delightful, as usual. Plenty of crisp lettuce, with the enormous slices of tomato common to the area. There were various salads, served in mayonnaise, stuffed eggs, sliced meats, lobster and *quiche*, and lots of white wine to wash it all down. The cheese and fruit were delicious, each providing a contrast, and there was ice cream for Nikos, and coffee for the rest.

Sylvie ate little, and she noticed that Andreas did not make a good meal either. Leon did, munching happily through every course, drinking the glass of wine he was allowed with evident relish, and obviously recovering a lot of his strength. Even his legs had lost their initial pallor, the darker pigment of his skin responding well to the sun's rays, and there was a little more flesh on his bones than when they arrived, pointing to the success of his recuperation.

Stephanos appeared after lunch to escort his employer to his room for a rest, and as Irene had already taken a drowsy Nikos for his sleep, Sylvie and Andreas were left alone at the table.

'I gather you have not adopted the habit of sleeping the afternoon hours away,' he remarked, after Irene had cleared all but their coffee cups.

'You know I haven't,' she retorted, her tone faintly irritable. 'What time do you expect Eleni to arrive?'

Andreas pushed back his chair and got abruptly to his feet. 'Why do you persist in asking about Eleni? What does it matter to you when she comes or how long she plans to stay?'

Because then I will know how long you plan to stay, Sylvie longed to answer, but she chose discretion and held her tongue.

When she didn't answer, Andreas looked down at her half impatiently, and then, with another change of mood, he said: 'How would you like to have some fun this afternoon? I know the ideal place.'

Sylvie caught her breath. 'But——'

'Eleni, I know,' he finished for her crisply. 'Well? Do you want to come or do you not? I need to get away from this place and I am asking you to come with me.'

'In the dinghy?' Sylvie was still doubtful

'No.' Andreas's lips tightened. 'We will sail the dinghy round to the harbour and pick up the yacht. I am prepared to believe that Leon knows more about the weather than I do.'

'But won't a yacht——'

'It is a motor cruiser,' Andreas interrupted her curtly. 'Do you come or not?'

Sylvie bit her lip. 'All right. I'll get changed——'

'Come as you are,' he retorted, crossing to the steps. 'Come! Time is wasting.'

The dinghy was easy to handle, and although Sylvie had never sailed before, she found it wasn't difficult to follow Andreas's instructions. He seemed to relax as they left the cove, and by the time they reached the harbour, he was laughing at her inexpert attempts to keep her balance, his hands warm and possessive on her body as he swung her up on to the dock.

The motor cruiser proved to be a forty-foot yacht with twin diesel engines, and berths for four to six people, depending on their needs. There was a luxurious forward cabin, and twin bunks in the bow, and a comprehensive living area that could convert to a further double bedroom. Sylvie was fascinated by the galley, and the heads, with their bath and shower facilities, and Andreas left her to her explorations while he took the craft out of the harbour.

On the open sea, the engines carried them along at quite a pace, and it was exhilarating to stretch out on the deck and allow the quickening breeze to keep her cool. She wished she had brought a swimsuit with her. She would have liked to dive overboard in these deep waters and practise more of her snorkelling, but she had to content herself with sunbathing, and be glad that at least what she was wearing was thin and practical.

When she eventually went aft to find out what Andreas was doing, she found him lounging lazily at the wheel, studying the charts laid out in front of him. 'Where are we going?' she asked, leaning rather impulsively over his shoulder, and he shifted slightly so that his shoulders did not come into contact with her breasts.

Immediately she drew back, feeling rather chastened, but his tone was casual as he indicated their destination on the map. 'It is an island called Stavira,' he replied, narrowing his eyes to gaze ahead. 'It is used almost exclusively by a travel club based in Athens, and there is usually plenty going on, whatever the time of day or night.'

'But——' Sylvie frowned, 'don't the locals mind?'

'There are no locals,' declared Andreas flatly. 'Except for one or two who run the *taverna* down by the jetty. It is a cosmopolitan resort, very brash and sophisticated, and what the people do there is their concern.'

Sylvie was intrigued, if a little apprehensive. But rather than cause another argument, she refrained from commenting, returning to her previous position on the deck, inhaling the pungent smell of the ocean, and refusing to contemplate Eleni's reactions when she arrived to find her fiancé missing.

The sound of guitars and the rhythmic beat of drums welcomed their arrival at Stavira. It was the kind of place Sylvie had never expected to find so far from the mainland, but Andreas had been right, it was brash and noisy, and the source of the music was quickly identified as coming from a barbecue party on the beach.

'Can anyone join in?' asked Sylvie doubtfully, as

Andreas tied up the yacht and held out his hand towards her, and he grinned at her wryly as they walked between the tables of an outdoor restaurant.

'Providing you buy a few drinks,' he assured her lightly, acknowledging the greeting of a white-coated waiter. 'It is only an hotel, Sylvie, even though it calls itself the Club Athénée. A rather modern establishment, frequented generally by the younger section of the tourist population.'

Apart from the *taverna*, on the waterfront, the hotel did indeed seem to be the island's only habitation, Sylvie realised. A sprawling multi-storied building, it occupied the prime position on the rise just above the beach, with strategically planted palm trees surrounding pools and tennis courts. There were signs for beauty salons and massage parlours beside others indicating the pools and restaurants, but the atmosphere was cosmopolitan as Andreas had said, and Sylvie thought she much preferred Monastiros, which was essentially Greek.

Andreas seemed in a strange mood, and she was not entirely at ease with him as they descended the steps to the beach. There was a brittleness about him, a sense of hard determination, and her apprehensions were not eased to discover that many of the women present wore only their bikini briefs.

Almost immediately Andreas was hailed by a group of people gathered around the bar which had been set up along side the barbecue spits. There were perhaps ten or twelve men and women, their ages ranging from early twenties to late thirties, all in swimwear, and all appearing to Sylvie as some exotic tribe from another planet. The women particularly wore a lot of make-up, but the men vied with them when it came to jewellery, sporting rings and pendants, and even ear-rings in one case.

There were no formal introductions. Sylvie was announced as Sylvie, and Andreas mentioned one or two names in passing. But apart from several curious glances, none of the women were interested in her, and Sylvie felt totally out of her depth with the men.

'*Chéri*,' one of the women addressed Andreas in drawling tones, 'it has been an age since we have seen you. Where have you been hiding yourself? You know what they say, all work and no play . . .'

'Perhaps the fair Eleni has been digging in her claws,' remarked an exquisite-looking blonde, wearing a skimpy white G-string, and a bra that was scarcely decent. Whereas the first woman had definitely had a French accent, the blonde was evidently English, and she regarded Sylvie with sympathetic amusement.

'It doesn't look as if he's been short of company anyway,' observed a thin young man, in pale blue briefs. 'Who is Sylvia, that's what we all want to know. Come on, Andreas, have you taken to baby-snatching?'

Sylvie flushed, and turned away to watch the musicians and the other holidaymakers, all seemingly enjoying themselves, either dancing or plunging into the sea to cool off. There was much talk and laughter, and the sizzling sound of steaks on the grid, but she wished herself far away from this noisy beach.

'Do you want to dance?'

The young male voice with its definitely English accent was not unattractive, and Sylvie blinked and tried to concentrate on the young man who had addressed her. He was not one of the group surrounding Andreas, who she saw was laughingly endeavouring to explain his reasons for being there, and he looked nice, and friendly, and glad of the diversion, she nodded.

It was good to be active, to dance to the disco music, and forget her discomfort at the hands of Andreas's 'friends'. Somehow she didn't think they were the usual crowd he went around with, but just a fringe element of the same, but for some reason he had felt the need for their company, and had brought her along for the ride. She wished he hadn't. She wished she was back on Monastiros, having afternoon tea with Leon, and discussing the events of the day. Life seemed so uncomplicated there, or at least it had until Andreas appeared. Now she doubted her life would ever be so uncomplicated again, and the ball of depression swelled inside her as she contemplated going back to England and never seeing him again.

She became aware suddenly that Andreas had stopped what he was doing and was watching her, a brooding expression on his dark face. She hoped he didn't object to her accepting her partner's offer to dance. After all, he had been occupied, and at least the young man, whose name she had discovered was Roger, wasn't trying to make a pass at her as soon as he had a chance.

She quivered though when Andreas parted from the group, until she saw that the blonde girl was behind him. A few yards from where Sylvie and Roger were dancing, Andreas stopped and drew the girl into his arms, and they began to move sinuously to the music. It was hardly dancing, just an excuse to put their arms around one another, and Sylvie's face burned when the girl twined her fingers in his hair and turned her mouth up for his kiss.

'Do you mind if we stop now?'

Sylvie turned away abruptly, giving Roger an apologetic smile as she stumbled across the packed sand. But she couldn't bear to go on watching such an intimate display, and she felt a little sick and dizzy, which she told herself was the heat.

'Let me get you a drink,' exclaimed Roger eagerly, his young face creased with anxiety. 'You look awfully pale. Have a Coke. You're probably dehydrated.'

'Thanks.'

Sylvie was grateful, and she was standing staring determinedly out to sea when Roger came back. 'Here.' He handed her a bottle of Pepsi. 'Now, tell me all about yourself.'

Sylvie shook her head. 'There's nothing to tell.'

'I don't believe it. Who was that guy you came with? Your uncle? Your brother?'

'My—brother-in-law,' admitted Sylvie carefully.

'I knew it,' Roger grinned. 'I knew he was too old to be your boy-friend.'

'But not old enough to be my father?' suggested Sylvie tensely.

'I wouldn't have thought so.' Roger glanced round. 'Who's the blonde?'

'You tell me.' Sylvie was abrupt, and Roger nodded his head as if he understood.

'I get it. You're worried about what your sister will think if she finds out he's been fooling around,' he exclaimed.

'What? Oh——' Sylvie pressed her lips together half hysterically. 'Oh, yes. Yes, that's right. I'm worried about that.'

'I thought you were. Gee——' Roger turned to stare again, 'he's with a redhead now. He's some swinger, your brother-in-law.'

'Yes, isn't he?' Sylvie was growing tired of this ridiculous conversation. 'If—if you'll excuse me, I think I'd better be getting back.'

'To the hotel?'

'Oh, no.' She shook her head. 'We're not staying here.'

'You're not?'

'No, she is not,' averred a harsh voice that Sylvie recognised only too well. 'Come, *pethi mou*, it is time we were leaving. It is nearly six o'clock.'

Sylvie swung round mutinously. 'Are you sure you're

ready?' she exclaimed. 'Don't let me spoil your fun.' She looked defiantly at Roger. 'I'm enjoying myself.'

'Now,' said Andreas bleakly, his hand fastening round her wrist. 'Say goodbye to your—friend. I do not wish to argue about it.'

Sylvie grimaced apologetically at Roger, then allowed Andreas to compel her across the sand to the steps. She noticed the younger man made no attempt to argue with Andreas either, and although she had not been attracted to him, she reflected that Andreas made him look rather immature. Nevertheless, she resented his arbitrary behaviour, and tore herself away once they were back on board the yacht.

'Excuse me, but why did you bring me along?' she asked sarcastically, rubbing her reddening wrist as he started the powerful engines. 'And was that display of brute aggression really necessary? I thought you seemed to be having a whale of a time!'

Andreas ignored her, concentrating on negotiating the craft away from the dock, but Sylvie wasn't to be silenced. 'You have no right to treat me like that!' she declared, sniffing resentfully. 'Roger must have thought I was a complete idiot!'

'I apologise.'

Andreas's words were as unexpected as his behaviour had been, and she gulped. 'You're sorry?'

'What more do you want me to say?' He swung the wheel expertly, and pressed the release valves forward. 'Take a look at the sky. It is not so pretty now, is it? I hope we may get back before the storm breaks.'

Sylvie looked up, at a loss for words, and saw what he meant. The blueness was overlaid with a film of sulphurous cloud, giving the sky an oppressive appearance, yellow and threatening.

'Is it going to thunder?' asked Sylvie, looping her leg

over the leather seat opposite his where he was seated at the wheel.

'Why?' Andreas looked sideways at her. 'Does thunder frighten you?'

Sylvie compressed her lips for a moment. 'No,' she said at last. 'But lightning does. Is it going to be bad?'

Andreas shrugged. 'It may pass over. I have seen such clouds, without a drop of rain falling.'

'That doesn't reassure me.' Sylvie could imagine an electrical storm without rain. She bent her head. 'We shouldn't have come.'

Andreas looked at her again. 'That I would endorse.'

'So why did we?' Sylvie hunched her shoulders. 'I though you were enjoying yourself.'

'With Celia? Oh, yes.' His tone was harsh. 'She is—how would you say—a good sport.'

'I'll bet.' Sylvie cupped her chin on her hand and turned to stare out of the side windows of the steering cabin.

'What is that supposed to mean?' Andreas was not amused.

'Nothing.' Sylvie shrugged. She did not want to start an argument with him here. 'It was quite a place, wasn't it? All—all those—women.'

'You were shocked?'

'No!' She gave him a brief scornful stare. 'I suppose you're used to it.'

'Why should you suppose that? Greek women do not disport themselves in such a way.'

'No.' Sylvie acknowledged the truth of this. 'Because you don't let them.'

Andreas's eyes darkened ominously. 'You think we should? Is this how you would wish to behave?'

'I didn't say that.' Sylvie seemed incapable of keeping out of deep water.

'So what are you saying?' Andreas persisted.

'Well, you didn't seem to object,' she exclaimed defensively.

'No.' Andreas stared broodingly ahead, over the increasingly choppy water. 'I have seen a woman's body before. It is no novelty.'

Sylvie's face burned. 'Have you seen Eleni's?' she blurted, before she could prevent herself, and cringed in total abjection beneath his contemptuous stare.

'You had better go below,' he declared, making no attempt to answer her. 'You will feel safer down there. As you can see, it is starting to rain, and I shall need all my concentration to keep the craft on course.'

Sylvie stumbled down the steps into the cabin, shivering from reaction. But not because of the expected vehemence of the storm. Somehow lightning seemed a paltry thing compared to Andreas's suppressed violence, and she seated herself unhappily on the edge of the banquette, wondering what had happened to make everything go so desperately wrong.

She was so sunk in misery she was hardly aware of the passage of time, but when she heard the engines slowing she was forced to turn her head. The sight of an island only a few yards away across a rain-tossed expanse of water made her blink disbelievingly, and she knelt on the cushioned seat and stared out incredulously, hardly able to comprehend that they were back already.

Andreas's voice calling her name distracted her, however, and she turned, putting one leg to the floor as he appeared halfway down the flight of steps. 'Sylvie! Are you all right?'

'Yes, yes, I'm fine.' Sylvie put both feet to the floor. 'What is it? What's happened? Is this Monastiros?'

'Does it look like Monastiros?' he enquired dryly. 'We do not have jet engines, Sylvie. No, this is an uninhabited island, so far as I know. I have been trying to use the radio, but the reception is bad, so I have anchored here to try and make contact with Monastiros.' He paused. 'We do not want Leon to worry about us, do we?'

'Oh, no.' Sylvie swallowed rather convulsively. 'Th-thanks for letting me know.'

Andreas hesitated a moment, then he nodded and went back up the steps again. A few moments later she heard him using the two-way radio, the crackling on the air indicative of the electricity about in the atmosphere. It was thundering and lightning, but she had hardly been aware of it, and only now, anchored in this quiet cove, did she feel a return of her earlier apprehension.

Presently she realised Andreas must have made contact with somebody. He was speaking in his own language, but not the same words over and over again as before. This time he was evidently describing their position, reassuring whoever was in contact with him that they were in no danger. She sighed. What a disastrous afternoon it had turned out to be, after the success of the previous day. They should have been reversed, she thought unhappily. Andreas should have been left with a good opinion of her, not this awful aggression between them.

'Success!' His exclamation broke into her brooding reverie, and she turned from her contemplation of the rain driving against the portholes to look at him blankly. 'I made it,' he said patiently. 'I got through to the coastguard at Siros, and he will relay the message to the villa.'

'Oh! Oh, good!' Sylvie forced a faint smile. 'Thank heavens for radios.'

Andreas nodded. 'Indeed.' He came down the last few steps into the cabin. 'Are you really all right? You seem—pale—withdrawn.' He sighed. 'I guess I am to blame for this also.'

Sylvie expelled her breath uneasily. 'No—at least, I shouldn't have said what I did. It was impertinent.

What—what you choose to do is no concern of mine. I'm sorry.'

Andreas's mouth twisted. 'You were right, I should not have brought you with me. It was selfish.'

'Selfish?'

'Of course.' He thrust his hands into the hip pockets of the denim shorts. 'I have no right to take advantage of you like this.'

'Take advantage of me?' Sylvie was confused. 'I don't understand——'

'Yes, you do.' He bent his head broodingly, scuffing his bare toe against the floorboards. 'I should have left you at the villa. You and I—our relationship is not sensible.'

'Sensible?' Sylvie couldn't help repeating everything he said. 'Andreas——'

'Andreas, Andreas! Even the way you say my name is a provocation,' he muttered, looking at her with eyes that were no longer dark, but smouldering like red-hot coals. 'Oh, Sylvie, why in God's name do I want you!'

She did not have time to consider these words. In a couple of strides he had erased the space between them, and she was looking up into his dark face. With studied deliberation he put his hands on her waist and pulled her up against him, and then, as her eyes widened half in apprehension, he bent his head and covered her lips with his.

It was a hard kiss, but not intimate, her own nervous tension causing her to clench her teeth, so that her lips were bruised against them. When he lifted his head there was a faintly rueful twist to his mouth, but he did not release her, only looked at her with narrow-eyed intentness.

'You can do better than that,' he said accusingly. 'But perhaps it is safer this way. I do not want to hurt you, Sylvie, but I fear I am in danger of doing so.'

'H-how—hurt me, I mean?' she articulated chokily, and his hands slid from her waist, beneath the hem of her vest to spread against the soft skin covering her spine.

'Like this,' he answered, removing one hand to loosen the knots that held the vest in place. Sylvie's hand clutched convulsively at the cloth, but his eyes were compelling, and after a moment she let go, allowing him to expose her breasts. They were hard and firm, the nipples rose-tipped and pointed, and she quivered uncontrollably when he lowered his head and took one between his lips.

'No—I mean—you mustn't——' she got out unsteadily, but the persuasive caress of his tongue was contradicting all her previous convictions. Dear God, she thought dizzily, I want him to do this all over me, and when he trailed his lips across her throat and found hers again, her mouth opened eagerly, inviting his sensuous possession.

She was breathtakingly close to him, his leg between hers making her unmistakably aware of every muscle in his body. Yet even the few clothes they had on seemed an unbearable barrier, and her trembling fingers found the button of his shorts with instinctive urgency.

'Sylvie——' he groaned, pressing her hands against his body. 'Oh, Sylvie, what are you doing? You know what will happen if you go any further.'

'I know,' she breathed, blind to anything but her own hungry emotions. 'You wanted to see me. I want to see you. Why shouldn't I? Don't you want me to?'

'*Theos*—yes! Yes, of course I want you to,' he muttered thickly, releasing his fingers, but as she pressed the zipper downwards they heard a man's voice from somewhere above their heads.

Immediately Sylvie's hand froze, and with a smothered oath Andreas let her go, fastening his shorts again with grim determination and making automatically for the steps.

'The radio,' he said shortly, over his shoulder, and as her whole body sagged with stark reaction she realised someone was calling them on the frequency Andreas had used to contact Siros.

He came back perhaps five minutes later, but it could have been hours as far as Sylvie was concerned. In the gloom of the cabin, with the rain easing slowly outside, she was numb to anything but a sense of chilled rejection, the weakness of her knees finding expression in her shuddering agitation. With trembling fingers she tied the straps of the cotton vest again, and rescued the leather thong that had bound her hair from where it had fallen, on the floor. When Andreas returned she was standing ghostlike in the centre of the cabin, gazing at him apprehensively as he came barefoot down the stairs.

'It was Leon,' he said flatly, one hand resting lightly on the polished wood balustrade. 'They had patched him through from Monastiros. He was concerned. He thought we had taken the dinghy, and been forced ashore to make the call.' He paused, glancing up the steps behind him, as if already eager to be gone. 'I told him we were on the yacht, and that we were in no danger, and he expects us back within the hour.'

'I see.' Sylvie could not look at him. She felt too awful, too embarrassed. Oh, God, how could she have been so— so promiscuous, so utterly wanton! He probably imagined he wasn't the first man who had tried to make love to her, and no doubt she would not have stopped him if the radio call had not interrupted them.

Andreas hesitated. 'Eleni is with him,' he added. 'She arrived a couple of hours ago. Leon told her the storm must have delayed us, so we can be grateful for that, at least.'

You can, thought Sylvie mutely, the bitterness of jealousy like a twisting knife inside her. The idea of Andreas doing to Eleni what he had just done to her was an intolerable conception, and she turned away from him abruptly, crossing her arms across her body and gripping her elbows tightly.

'Sylvie!'

She had expected him to leave her, and she was not prepared for the sudden gentleness in his voice.

'Sylvie!' When she did not respond, he said her name again, and this time she managed a muffled: 'What?' when she recognised the trace of impatience he was trying hard to disguise.

'Do you want me to apologise?' he demanded, expelling his breath heavily. 'I warned you I might hurt you, and I have.'

'You haven't!' Sylvie could not bear to think that he might be pitying her. Swinging round, she faced him bravely, ignoring her hot cheeks as she challenged his troubled stare. 'I'm only sorry we were interrupted. The situation was just getting interesting, wasn't it?' She tilted her head. 'Pity we have a deadline now, isn't it?'

Andreas's dark brows descended, and he studied her provocative face for several minutes before turning abruptly and remounting the stairs. He said nothing, neither agreeing nor disputing her claim, and Sylvie maintained her defiance so long as he was in view, before sinking down weakly on to the banquette.

Andreas had driven the car down to the harbour that morning, when he took out the dinghy, and it was by this means that he drove Sylvie back to the villa. It had stopped raining by the time they reached Monastiros, and in the remarkable way of such storms, the clouds were already clearing, leaving an expanse of star-studded velvet above the luminous glow of the sunset.

They had not spoken since that moment on the yacht,

but Sylvie had no wish to break the silence. While she could maintain an indifferent façade, she had a deep well of misery inside her, and had Andreas chosen to breach her shell, he would have discovered the depths of the pain he had inflicted.

The lights were on in the villa as they drove up the track, and as Andreas parked the car near the garages at the back of the building, two people came strolling round the side of the house. It was Leon and Eleni, and Sylvie's nerves tightened automatically, as she prepared herself to face their comments.

'All right?' asked Andreas, in an undertone, as she turned to push open her door as soon as the wheels had stopped turning. His instinctive courtesy was almost her undoing. For a heart-stopping moment she knew an uncontrollable impulse to throw herself upon his mercy and let him do with her as he willed. But then Leon was pulling her door open, and his affectionate greeting destroyed the initiative.

'*Lipon*, you are back! *Oriste*, Sylvie, we have been so worried!'

'There was no need.' Sylvie's words came out jerkily, as she climbed out of the car, and Eleni paused to give her only the briefest of acknowledgements before hurrying round the vehicle to reach Andreas.

'*Agapitos!* Darling!' Eleni grasped Andreas's arm as he got out of the car, and once again Sylvie was subjected to the sight of another woman tilting her face for his kiss. Turning abruptly away, she allowed Leon to escort her round the villa, and up the shallow steps to the terrace, where Thia Ariadne was seated with her interminable lacework.

'Ah, *thespinis*, you are back,' she greeted the girl warmly. 'What a storm in a teacup, *ohi*? Is that not what you say? Ha, Leon, he has been like the hot kettle, ever since the storm broke.'

'I think you mean a hot cat, *thia*,' Leon corrected her dryly, but his smile was indulgent. 'Come, Sylvie, sit down. Let me get you a drink. I am sure you must be exhausted.'

Sylvie allowed herself to be seated, but she watched Leon anxiously. 'Are you sure you should be doing so much?' she exclaimed, glancing behind her apprehensively and discovering that Andreas and Eleni had not yet come to join them. 'Leon, don't be too ambitious, will you? Not when things seem to be going so well.'

'I won't.' Leon bent over her affectionately, touching her cheek with his fingers, and Sylvie thought rather wearily that Andreas would have to choose that moment to appear right behind them.

'So much concern, brother,' he remarked cuttingly. 'One wonders how you might have felt had it been Eleni, and not Sylvie, who was with me.'

If Leon was disturbed by his brother's unexpected sarcasm, he quickly hid it, and it was Eleni whose brows arched delicately, her eyes moving to Sylvie in evident surprise.

'Naturally I was concerned about Sylvie,' retorted Leon mildly, straightening to face the other man. 'She is my responsibility.'

'Is she?' Sylvie was amazed at Andreas's behaviour. It was as if he was blaming Leon for what had happened to them. 'I wonder what Margot would have to say about that?'

'Oh, really——'

Sylvie sprang up from her seat in sudden agitation, but it was Thia Ariadne who rose without any apparent haste and insinuated herself between the two brothers.

'I think that is enough, do you not?' she enquired, her calm tone tempered with steel. 'Andreas, you need to change. I do not propose to eat dinner with someone

wearing *shorts!*' Her lips curled distastefully. 'As for you,
Leon, I suggest you allow Sylvie to go and change also.
She has obviously had a trying afternoon. Do not assist in
making it an impossible evening.'

'*Ne*, Thia Ariadne.'

Leon accepted his aunt's advice without another word,
and although Andreas still looked dangerous, he strode
into the villa without further argument. Sylvie, for her
part, felt hopelessly out of her depth, and Eleni's eyes
upon her held none of the shy reticence Sylvie remembered from their first encounter.

But once again Ariadne came to the rescue. 'Run along,
little one,' she advised her gently, resuming her seat and
her sewing. 'We will wait dinner for you.' And Sylvie
offered Leon an apologetic shrug before doing as his aunt
suggested.

In her room, however, she found her legs giving out on
her again. What had Andreas been thinking of, causing
that scene on the terrace? How could he pick an argument
with his brother, knowing that Leon should not get upset?
And Eleni—what must she have thought? Was there no
end to the humiliation Sylvie was to suffer at his hands?

CHAPTER TEN

SYLVIE was awakened by the sound of the helicopter. It seemed to be directly overhead, but that was because sound travelled great distances over the water, and she crawled up on to her pillows, blinking at her watch.

She had not slept until the first faint fingers of dawn light touched the horizon, but although the sun was glinting through the shutters, she did not think it was very late. The air was still too cool, her bedroom too fresh, and she concentrated with difficulty until the watch face swam into focus.

As she had suspected, it was barely eight o'clock, and she pushed back the sheet which was all that was covering her and padded to the windows. The helicopter had gone now, the sound fading away into the distance, and she decided it must have been on its way to one of the other islands, and not their concern at all.

However, she was awake now, and the idea of going back to bed did not appeal at all. After only a moment's hesitation she pulled off her nightgown and replaced it with a bikini, and letting herself out of her bedroom, went barefoot down the stairs.

To her astonishment, someone had already had breakfast. Two places had been laid and discarded, and she was fingering the handle of the coffee pot doubtfully when she heard someone coming. Her heart pounded, as she anticipated what she would do if it proved to be Andreas, but to her relief it was Leon whose sandals flopped across the patio, his smile as warm as usual, as he took in the entrancing picture she made.

'*Kalimera*,' he hailed her easily, and she returned the

greeting, gesturing rather awkwardly at the evidence in front of her.

'Someone's beaten us to it,' she said, running her palms down over her honey-brown thighs. 'I can't believe it was Nikos, even if he was eager to see me last night.'

'It was Andreas,' Leon informed her wryly, taking a seat and stretching his legs. 'He phoned for the helicopter before he went to bed, and he and Eleni left half an hour ago.'

'Left?' Sylvie could hear the consternation in her voice, but Leon seemed not to notice.

'I am afraid so,' he confirmed, inhaling deeply. 'He decided he had to get back. It was a pity for Eleni, of course, but she would not stay without him, and perhaps it is just as well.'

Sylvie half turned away, breathing shallowly, struggling to contain her desolation. Andreas had gone! Just like that, he had gone! And she was sensitive enough to his moods to know that he would not be coming back.

'Is something wrong?' Leon was speaking to her, and she had to force herself to turn and face him again.

'I—no. No, what could be wrong? I—I was just watching that seabird, that's all. Isn't it enormous?'

'It looks like a pelican,' remarked Leon indifferently, crossing his legs. 'Would you ring the bell for Irene? She should have cleared this table by now.'

'Oh, yes.' Sylvie obediently summoned the maid, and then walked to the edge of the patio. 'I—er—I was just going for a swim. Will you excuse me? This—this is my favourite time of day.'

Leon hesitated. 'Last night—what Andreas said—it did not upset you, did it?'

Sylvie stiffened, but she had to look round. 'Last night?' she said, playing for time. 'I don't know what you mean.'

'I mean what he said to me,' declared Leon. 'About—

well, about our relationship. I do feel responsible for you, Sylvie, and I am very fond of you.'

Sylvie forced a smile. 'I know you are.'

'And were I not married to Margot——'

'Oh, Leon, don't go on.' Sylvie couldn't bear it. 'I'm going for a swim.' She stepped down on to the sand. 'See you later!'

A week later Sylvie had convinced herself that she would get over Andreas. She had to. There was nothing else she could do. But the spring had gone out of her walk, and she no longer felt the zest for living that had previously put vitality into her smile. It was harder to get up in the mornings, and harder to keep cheerful throughout the day, and what had been a joy and a pleasure to her before was now just so much time she had to get through, until she could return to England.

She and Leon had discussed her return to England. The day after Andreas's departure, Sylvie had gone to him and explained that whatever happened, she could not stay indefinitely.

'I don't know what story Margot told you,' she said uncomfortably, 'but I have to be back before the start of the Michaelmas term, in time to prepare myself and the things I have to take when I start university.'

'I knew that.' Leon was endearingly understanding. 'Andreas told me that you were just filling in, and I know he has another girl in mind, who will take over from you when you want to leave.'

Sylvie's lips had tightened. She should have known Andreas would have everything organised, she thought bitterly. It wasn't any part of his nature to leave himself unprotected.

The nights were the worst, naturally. After the household had retired, Sylvie no longer found it a simple matter to escape her thoughts in oblivion. She couldn't relax. She couldn't persuade her tense muscles to let go. And although she practised all the yoga exercises she had read about, nothing seemed to do any good.

In consequence, the silent hours between darkness and dawn assumed a nightmare quality, and she dreaded them coming with all the fervency of a toddler afraid of the dark. She looked at her watch a dozen times throughout the long hours, each time disbelieving how little time had passed since the last time she took notice.

One thing, she told herself, she was grateful for. The extra weight she had always carried on her hips and thighs fell away, leaving her as thin and bony as Margot had ever been. It was amazing how quickly weight disappeared when one was not eating or sleeping well, she reflected, and she wondered if she should write to some slimmers' magazine, and recommend insomnia as a diet.

She thought Leon had begun to worry about her too, and although she wanted to allay his anxieties, there was not a lot she could do. Besides, he was growing stronger every day, and the doctor who came from Athens to visit his patient pronounced that he was well on the way to recovery. That morning, the morning the helicopter arrived bringing the doctor from the mainland, Sylvie had waited in nervous anticipation for Andreas to appear. But only Dr Maxwell arrived at the villa, accompanied by his nurse, and Sylvie dug sand castles on the beach, with a determination born of desperation.

She had written back to her mother and Margot, but so far she had received no replies. The post on Monastiros was not regular, and in consequence she was not troubled when no letters arrived for her. Although she was looking forward to going home and forgetting what had happened here, the idea of picking up her studies again also seemed alien to her, and she put off thinking of the inevitable outcome.

It was funny, she thought, but when she came to Greece the idea of giving up her plans for a career would have seemed totally unreasonable. Now, however, it was the prospect of academic life that seemed cold and bleak, and she realised how much less important qualifications were than people. Her mother had always maintained that she was the one who had the brains, but that Margot's beauty was sufficient compensation. It was Margot who was expected to marry well, and had done so, while she, Sylvie, had never ever imagined herself in a situation like this. Her dealings with Brian, and boys like him, had confirmed her conviction that she was incapable of any deep emotional upheaval, and to find herself as weak and as vulnerable as any other girl was both chastening and terrifying. She didn't want to feel this way about Andreas. She didn't want to care about him, or wonder where he was and who he was with. She didn't want to spend the rest of her life wishing for something that was out of reach. Andreas was a man, he was too old for her, and he was already committed to someone else. Besides, he had admitted, he could only hurt her.

For once, however, what she wanted didn't seem to make any difference. No matter how she tried to avoid it, no matter that she tried to close her ears to the facts, the truth was ringing in her head. She was in love with Andreas. She cared desperately for someone who had found her just an amusing diversion. And although she would not admit it, there was no way out.

But in consequence, with characteristic determination she set about convincing herself that she would get over it. It might take time, years even, but sooner or later she would forget about him. Or if not forget, at least be able to think about him without this awful sense of desolation.

No one died of love, she told herself severely. They only wilted a little. Nevertheless, her health did deteriorate, and at the end of another week Leon spoke to her gently, suggesting in his apologetic way that perhaps she ought to go home.

'I do not quite know how to phrase this, Sylvie,' he said, as they sat over coffee after dinner one evening. Thia Ariadne had retired to her balcony and they were alone, and he covered her hand with his as he sought the right words.

'I want you to know how much I appreciate you giving up your time to come here. No——' This as Sylvie would have protested, 'I know you are going to say it has been in the nature of a holiday for you, but nonetheless, you came when I was at my lowest ebb, and helped me to get my life into perspective again.'

Sylvie forced a smile. 'Honestly, Leon, I've done nothing.'

'On the contrary,' he was adamant, 'you have done a great deal. Not only for me, but for Nikos, too. You have made him see that he can be happy, even without his mother.' He paused. 'You have made me see that, too.'

'Oh, Leon——'

'No, listen to me, Sylvie. I want you to know. When—when Andreas accused me of abusing my responsibilities towards you, I denied it——'

'Leon!'

'—but I fear it was not exactly true.'

'Please, Leon . . .'

'Let me finish.' He moistened his lips. 'Sylvie, these last days have convinced me that I must say something more. Watching you, worrying about you, seeing you fade away before my eyes, I knew I must be honest with you. I have come to care about you, Sylvie, to care about you very deeply. And if circumstances were different I should be proud to ask you to be my wife.'

'Oh, Leon . . .' Sylvie was appalled. She was not prepared for this. 'Leon, please, you don't understand . . .'

'What do I not understand?' Leon looked perplexed as she withdrew her hand from beneath his and got nervously to her feet. 'You cannot lie to me, Sylvie. We have lived together for six weeks, remember, and I have seen you changed from a vital, vivacious child into a hollow-eyed wraith of a woman. There can be only one reason for that change—me!' He pointed towards himself. 'Can you honestly tell me you do not care for me?'

'Of course not.' Sylvie turned to him helplessly, wringing her hands, caught in the cleft stick of her own emotions. 'Leon, of course I—I care for you——'

'I knew it!'

'—but as a brother! A brother! Only as a brother.'

Leon's brows descended. 'You are saying this for Margot's sake——'

'No!' Sylvie was desperate. 'Leon, I like you, I do. I think you're one of the nicest men I've ever met, but I don't love you—not in the way you mean. I'm sorry.'

Leon gazed at her uncomprehendingly. Obviously he needed some time to absorb this statement, and Sylvie turned away hopelessly, wanting to leave him. She didn't know how long she had before the real reason for her condition occurred to him, and she didn't think she could bear for him to offer her his sympathy.

'Then you must be homesick,' he said at last, his voice flat and expressionless, eloquent of the shock he had sustained. Sylvie prayed that her honesty would not be the prelude to a setback in his recovery, but for the moment it was enough to have something concrete to cling to.

'Yes,' she agreed hastily. 'Yes, I think I am. I—well, perhaps it would be best if I went home.'

'Home?' Leon looked at her bitterly. 'You mean—all this, this fretting you have been doing is just because you wish to go home?'

Sylvie sighed. 'Is it so—unlikely?'

'Yes!' With unexpected vehemence, Leon pronounced the denial. 'Sylvie, look at me. Look at me! If I am not responsible for those dark lines around your eyes, then it must be someone else, do you not agree?'

'Leon——'

He got to his feet, pushing back his chair and facing her with grim determination. 'I should have realised,' he declared savagely. 'I should have understood: only I regret, my illness has made my brain sluggish. *Theos!*' He smote his forehead with the flat of his hand. 'How could I have been so blind, so insensitive, so foolishly arrogant as to imagine I could have had such a devastating effect on you!'

'Please, Leon, leave it——'

'It is Andreas, is it not?' he demanded, somewhat wearily now as his anger drained his strength. 'What has he done to you? If he has hurt you, I will kill him!'

Sylvie uttered a slightly hysterical laugh. 'Leon, this is ridiculous! How could Andreas hurt me? Don't be silly.'

'I have not been silly, only conceited,' he declared harshly. 'Imagining your distress could have anything to do with me.' He shook his head. 'I understand now why my brother was so angry every time he found us together. Andreas can be very jealous of his possessions——'

'Leon, I'm not his possession!'

'No?' He studied her pale face. 'I wonder how well you know him.'

'Leon, he's your brother, that's all.'

'He has not—touched you?'

Sylvie bent her head. 'Not in the way you mean, no.'

'What way do I mean?' Leon was dogged.

'He—he hasn't—made love to me,' exclaimed Sylvie tremulously, not knowing why she was even answering his questions. 'Leon, don't ask me, please. It—it's over. It's all over.'

Leon's mouth compressed. 'I shall have much pleasure in telling him what I think of his behaviour——'

'Oh, no!' Sylvie was horrified. 'Leon, no! No, you mustn't. Whatever else you do, please don't mention any of this to Andreas.'

'He should know what he has done,' insisted Leon grimly, and Sylvie gazed at him in agony.

'Leon,' she appealed, 'if you—if you feel anything for me at all, promise me you'll never mention this to another living soul!'

Leon sighed. 'You ask the impossible, Sylvie.'

'Why? Why do I? Isn't it my affair? Not yours?'

Leon hunched his shoulders. 'I cannot understand any of this. It is not like Andreas to show disrespect to any of the female members of his family.'

'But I'm not of his family, am I?' Sylvie pointed out unsteadily. 'Leon, when do you want me to leave?'

'I do not want you to leave,' he replied simply. 'But if that is what you want, then you must do as you wish.'

'Thank you.' Sylvie expelled her breath heavily. 'I—I'll go on Monday, the day after tomorrow. Could you arrange for my flight from Athens?'

'Of course.' Leon inclined his head. 'My father will do it. I suppose you would rather it were he, and not Andreas?'

'Oh, yes,' Sylvie nodded. 'I'd rather Andreas knew nothing about it. I'd like to be gone before he finds out.'

Leon showed his understanding, and impulsively, Sylvie reached up and kissed his cheek. 'Margot is a fool,' she declared huskily, and hurried into the villa.

She was awakened once again by the sound of the helicopter, and she lay for several minutes listening to the whirring blades, wondering if Leon had betrayed her and telephoned his brother. But it was precipitate at least to imagine that Andreas could simply drop what he was doing and take a flight out to the island, even if he had some reason for objecting to her departure.

Realising she would have to find out, Sylvie slid hurriedly out of bed, and after a skimpy wash she dressed in shorts and a tee-shirt and went downstairs.

The landing pad was perhaps half a mile from the villa, but she couldn't imagine anyone's having driven out to meet the aircraft at this hour of the morning. It was barely eight o'clock, and even Nikos had not yet put in an appearance.

Irene appeared as she was faltering on the patio, wondering what she should do, and she turned to the Greek woman eagerly, using her small knowledge of the language, combined with certain miming actions, to ascertain the reasons for the helicopter's arrival.

'Not know, *kyria*,' Irene exclaimed apologetically, spreading her hands in evident confusion. 'Perhaps doctor?' she suggested, with an expressive grimace, and Sylvie nodded her agreement as her own thoughts ran along the same lines. 'You like—*kafes*?'

'Coffee? Oh, yes, please, Irene.' Sylvie smiled. '*Parakalo.*'

'*Poli kala, kyria.*'

The Greek woman left her, and Sylvie moved impatiently to the low wall surrounding the patio, where the blossoms spilled their scarlet petals. The doctor would be here directly. Surely her talk with Leon last evening had not produced a crisis. Yet what other reason could the doctor have for arriving at this early hour, when on that other occasion it had been almost noon?

'My God, this climate! How did I stand it?'

The drawling words and the sudden throbbing of the

helicopter's propellers overhead occurred simultaneously. Sylvie's eyes were automatically drawn upwards, but she swung round on her heels towards the sound of that voice, and as her gaze lowered she caught her breath. A woman was standing at the top of the steps leading from the courtyard at the back of the building, slim and exotic in a scarlet jumpsuit, fanning herself with a navy clutch bag.

'Margot!' Sylvie's lips framed the word as her sister caught sight of her, and the older girl's lips compressed impatiently as she took in Sylvie's astonishment.

'Couldn't you have sent the car to meet me?' she exclaimed, advancing across the terrace. 'Even at this hour of the morning I could have done without a ten-mile hike! What on earth were you thinking of? Dreaming, as usual!'

Sylvie tried to gather her scattered senses. 'It's not a ten-mile hike, Margot. It's barely half a mile. And how was I to know you were in the helicopter? I—I thought it was the doctor.'

'Why?' Margot's thin brows ascended. 'Oh, don't tell me Leon's sick again. I couldn't bear it, not after everything else.'

'You couldn't bear it?' Sylvie could feel her voice rising, but she controlled it abruptly, realising it was not up to her to criticise Margot. She was here—that was the important thing. At least it would make her departure that much easier when the time came.

'Is there anything to drink? I'm parched!'

Margot lounged into a chair just as Irene reappeared with Sylvie's coffee, and the Greek woman stared at the newcomer with unconcealed admiration. 'Er—this is Kyrios Leon's wife——' began Sylvie, only to have Margot interrupt her rudely, saying: 'Pour me some coffee, there's a love. And ask her to fetch another cup, would you?'

Irene did not seem to notice the snub, and with a gesture of helplessness Sylvie gave Margot her cup and filled it with coffee. 'Thanks,' said Margot, sipping it eagerly. 'Oh, well, at least I've got here, which is something, I suppose.'

'You've come—to stay?' Sylvie was loath to ask the question, but Margot merely nodded.

'Regrettably,' she drawled, her lips twisting sardonically. 'I'm out of the play, darling, isn't it a drag? And Mummy simply refused to support me any longer.'

Sylvie stared at her. 'You're—*out* of the play?'

'That's what I said.' Margot sniffed discontentedly. 'So now I suppose I've got to get used to this place again.'

Sylvie blinked. 'I don't understand. You mean the play has folded?'

'No, darling, I mean I'm out.' Margot's tone was brittle. 'Don't you understand perfect English any more? I'm out! Sacked! Fired! Give it any definition you will. My acting career is over.'

Sylvie gulped. 'But why?'

Margot sighed. 'I suppose you could call it a conflict of personalities.'

'You—and who else?'

'The director, darling.' Margot expelled her breath impatiently. 'Oh, well, I suppose you won't be satisfied until you know all the sordid details. He thought he had control of me, as well as the play. I—disillusioned him.'

Sylvie shook her head. 'He made a pass at you?'

'Your vocabulary!' Margot laughed rather scornfully. 'My child, directors don't make "passes". They—well, they have much more subtle ways than that. But of course you wouldn't know.'

'No.' Sylvie bent her head. 'So you decided to come back.'

'Yes. I'm sorry to chase you off, darling, but you know

how it is. Beggars can't be choosers!'

Sylvie bit her lip. 'I'd have thought you'd do anything to keep that part.'

'Sylvie!' Margot looked genuinely shocked. 'What has Leon been teaching you?'

'I simply meant that if you were so keen to become a successful actress you might have considered adulterating your principles now and then,' declared Sylvie flatly. 'Or do you love Leon, after all?'

'Adulterating my principles!' Margot gasped. 'Heavens, Sylvie, what do you know about such things?'

Sylvie shrugged. 'Not a lot. But sleeping with somebody—that doesn't seem such a great price to pay.'

Margot gazed at her as if she had never seen her before. 'How would you know? You've never slept with anybody. And let me tell you, it's not all that it's cracked up to be!'

Sylvie felt the hot colour invade her cheeks. 'Isn't it?'

Margot frowned. 'Leon hasn't—you didn't——'

'No, of course not, Margot!' Sylvie was contemptuous. 'But you couldn't have blamed us if we had. You obviously cared nothing for his illness.'

'My, my!' Margot shook her head. 'You have grown up, haven't you, Sylvie? And lost weight, too, if I'm not mistaken. Who is it? Some lusty Greek fisherman, all brawn and no brains?'

'It is Andreas, actually,' declared Leon's quiet voice behind them, and Sylvie's lips parted in pained disbelief. 'I am sorry, little one,' he added apologetically, 'but somehow I do not think Margot will betray your secret.' He turned to his wife who was gazing at Sylvie incredulously. 'It was Andreas *you* wanted in the first place, was it not, Margot? Only he was too shrewd to be taken in by your selfish wiles. And it must be said, he would never have allowed you to make a fool of him, as you have made of me!'

CHAPTER ELEVEN

'SYLVANA, I am sorry to have to say this, but—well, we have been disappointed in you. Your results this far have been quite deplorable, and I am told you have developed the habit of absenting yourself from lectures mentally, if not physically. This is not what we expected of someone with your academic record, Sylvana. Not what we expected at all.'

'I am sorry.' Sylvie wriggled up a little higher in her chair, facing her tutor across his desk with wide-eyed candour, yet revealing nothing of her inner feelings.

'Is that all you have to say?' Professor Hutchins was being very patient. 'No words of mitigation, no reasons for this sudden lack of communication?'

Sylvie shook her head.

'But you must have.' The elderly tutor was trying to pierce the shell that this particular student seemed to have built around herself. 'Is it a personal problem? Do you have difficulties at home? Is it money?'

'I don't have any personal problems, sir,' Sylvie shrugged. 'Perhaps you should expell me.'

Professor Hutchins was aghast. 'Is that what you want? To be expelled?'

Sylvie shook her head again. 'I don't know.'

'Sylvana!' He made a sound of frustration. 'I will not accept that there is no reason for your behaviour. Why, the headmaster at your last school couldn't speak too highly of you, and your results in your 'O' and 'A' level examinations more than justified the faith he had in you.' He sighed. 'Something has happened, hasn't it?

Something that has nothing to do with school or university. But what? What?'

'Can I go now?' Sylvie slid off her chair, standing before him, slim and fragile in jeans and sweat-shirt. She looked like the quintessential student, he thought ruefully, but she was no use to him.

'I think we must leave this for now,' he declared, shifting her papers together. 'After Christmas we'll pursue this again. But for the present, have a good holiday, and try and come back to us in a different frame of mind.'

Sylvie smiled, but as she let herself out of the Professor's room her smile disappeared. She had tried, she thought, unshed tears burning at the backs of her eyes. But whatever she did, she couldn't concentrate. Even after more than four months Andreas still filled her thoughts to the exclusion of all else, and the idea of continuing with her education was ludicrous. She didn't feel like a student any longer, she felt like a woman, and the things she wanted could not be found in a lecture hall.

Conversely, they could not be found anywhere else either. She had neither seen nor heard anything of Andreas since she left Monastiros, and so far as she knew he could well be married to Eleni by now. Margot had not mentioned him in any of her letters, and Sylvie could hardly write and ask her sister for information. Now that she and Leon seemed to have settled their differences, and Nikos had a stable home life again, communication between the two families had reverted to its previous irregularity, and she knew her mother was simply delighted that all their problems seemed to be over.

There were a couple of letters waiting for her when she got back to the building where she had a room to herself. Taking them out of the rack, she turned them over uninterestedly in her hands, recognising her mother's handwriting on one, and unable to identify the sprawl on the other. Then her heart skipped a beat. The stamp on the strange letter was Greek, and so, too, was the postmark. Athens! *Athens!* She tore open the envelope.

It wasn't a long letter, just a dozen lines, but the signature was Andreas's. Dry-mouthed, she scanned the words he had written, and then had to read them again because she didn't take them in the first time.

Apparently he was in London, for a conference, and he wondered if she would like to have dinner with him on Friday evening. He was staying at the Savoy, and she could leave a message there, any time during the day or night.

Realising she was shaking quite badly now, Sylvie stumbled up the stairs to her room, and once inside, leant back weakly against the door. She must not, she simply *must not* read more into this than he was implying, she told herself severely. It was a friendly letter, that was all. He was simply asking her to have dinner with him. Why, for all she knew, Eleni might be with him.

The remembrance of Eleni sobered her. Even if he was alone, he could still be married, and she had to ensure that she did not make a fool of herself and ruin a perfectly innocent invitation.

Today was Wednesday. That left two whole days between now and Friday evening. She didn't know how she was going to survive that long. After all these weeks and months, forty-eight hours seemed an interminable sentence.

She straightened away from the door and studied the letter again, held between her shaking fingers. She could take the afternoon train to London on Friday. That would save the necessity of going home first. She had no lectures on Friday afternoon, and besides, most of the students were preparing to go home the following Wednesday. Apart from the carol service on Monday evening, and various end-of-term concerts, she was going to be free for five or six weeks, and she wondered whether Andreas knew this, and how long he proposed to stay.

Such speculations were not conducive to relaxation, and pulling on her navy blue duffel coat over her jeans, she left the building again, in search of a callbox. She could have called from the pay-phone in the building, but the idea of anyone overhearing their conversation made her seek a more private method of communication.

She had a pocket full of change, but when the pips sounded the connection, and she spoke to the receptionist at the Savoy, it was to be told that Andreas was not in the hotel.

'Is this Miss Scott?' she asked, after Sylvie had made her inquiry. 'Miss Sylvana Scott?' And after Sylvie had confirmed that it was, she explained: 'Mr Petronides left you a message, Miss Scott. If you are agreeable, he will meet you in the foyer, at seven o'clock on Friday evening. Does that meet with your approval?'

Sylvie was feeling a little breathless, but she managed to acknowledge that it did. 'Seven o'clock,' she agreed, a little faintly, and put down the receiver again with accurate precision.

She met one of her fellow students, walking back to her room. Martin Elliot was studying English and History, just as she was, and he grinned in a friendly fashion and fell into step beside her.

'You look—odd,' he remarked, causing the colour to deepen in Sylvie's cheeks. 'Is something wrong? Did old Hutchins give you a grilling?'

Sylvie's lips tilted. 'Well, yes, he did, actually.'

'You don't seem very concerned about it.'

Sylvie sighed. 'Well, I am. But—oh, Martin, I don't think I'm cut out for an academic career.'

Martin frowned. 'What do you mean—you'd rather get a job, get married, what?'

Sylvie bent her head. 'I'd rather get married, yes.'

Martin sighed. 'I guess there's some bloke, isn't there?'

'How do you know that?'

'The way you act, the way you look. Besides, a girl like you need never be short of male companionship, need she?'

Sylvie laughed. 'Thank you.'

Martin grimaced. 'Don't pretend you don't know. I've seen the way you've dealt with my friends. There had to be a reason for all that aloofness. I could tell at a glance you weren't frigid.'

'Could you?' Sylvie laughed again, excitement bubbling up inside her. 'Oh, well, here we are.'

She looked up at the tall ivy-clad building, thrusting her hands more deeply into the pockets of her duffel coat. It was a cold evening, but she didn't feel it. There was a warm glow inside her, which would not be extinguished, and the shell she had built around her was melting in its heat.

She arrived at the Savoy at five minutes to seven, having spent at least half an hour in the ladies' waiting room at Paddington, fretting over her appearance. At the university, she wore mostly jeans and sweaters, with an occasional skirt for light relief. Her supply of suits and dresses, therefore, the kind of things one would wear to go out to dinner, was limited, and although she had been told that the outfit she was wearing looked sensational, she had definite doubts about its suitability.

It was a dress, a simple tawny-brown dress, that relied on its rather daring lines to attract the unwary eye. It was a dress Margot had bought and never worn, and Sylvie had taken it to the university in the hope that she might find some use for it. She hadn't. This was its first outing; and the wrap-over bodice, with its deep cleavage and

narrow bootlace straps, made her abysmally aware of her
lack of curves. Once it had fitted her, but now it hung
loosely on her over-slender figure, accentuating her youth,
and the hollows around her neck. Even the magnificent
tan she had acquired in the summer had faded, and she
kept her grey sheepskin jacket wrapped closely about her
as she entered the glittering foyer of the Savoy.

It was quite busy at that hour of the evening, with men
and women in evening dress greeting friends and ordering
taxis, or simply seated comfortably, watching the colourful
tableau. Sylvie wasn't quite sure how to proceed, and she
was sure the doorman suspected she was some kind of
interloper. Even with her hair swept up, she was obviously
out of place in such a sophisticated gathering, and she
knew a sudden impulse to turn tail and run.

'Hello.'

The greeting caught her unawares, and she swung
round anxiously to find the man she had come to meet
right behind her. But this was Andreas as she had not seen
him before—in a black velvet suit and waistcoat, the
frilled shirt above in pristine contrast to the dark texture
of his skin.

'Andreas!' Her lips parted nervously, revealing her even
white teeth. 'I—it's good to see you again. Th-thank you
for your letter.'

Andreas looked down at her intently, but although he
inclined his head in acknowledgement of her stumbling
introduction, he did not smile. His face seemed thinner
than she remembered, but just as disturbing to her peace
of mind, and she stood there irresolutely, wondering how
she could have imagined he required anything more than
her company at dinner.

'You have lost weight,' he said at last, and the way he
said it, it was almost an accusation.

Sylvie's uncertain smile came and went. 'Yes,' she

murmured. It was all she could think of. 'So have you.'

Andreas glanced about him half impatiently, as if resentful of the people who were milling about them, then said sharply; 'Where do you want to eat? I know several good restaurants in London, and the grill-room here is quite excellent.' He paused. 'Or we could have dinner in my suite.'

Sylvie quivered. 'Oh, yes,' she breathed. 'Yes, please. In your suite. I—well, I'm sure I'm not dressed to go to any expensive restaurant.'

Andreas's mouth twisted. 'You look perfectly all right to me,' he retorted. 'But if that is really what you wish . . .'

'It is,' Sylvie nodded jerkily. 'Thank you.'

'Do not thank me, Sylvie,' he retorted, a trace of irritation in his voice, which she identified instinctively. Was he already regretting the impulse to invite her here? she wondered. Had he remembered her differently from what she really was? Was he sorry for her? Was he disappointed in her? Oh, God, why had she come here? It was all a terrible mistake!

'This way,' he said, gripping her upper arm and urging her towards the bank of lifts, his fingers hard, even through the skin of her coat.

Sylvie hesitated. 'Are—are you sure you want to—to do this?' she stammered, looking up at him apprehensively. 'I mean—if you'd rather we just had a drink somewhere——'

'Do you not want to have dinner with me?' he countered tautly, his dark face stiff and controlled, and Sylvie's knees shook.

'Well—yes,' she got out unsteadily, and without another word he propelled her into the lift, pressing the button for his floor before anyone else could enter the cubicle.

With his eyes upon her, Sylvie was hopelessly reminded

of the day she had arrived in Athens, the day Andreas had taken her to his apartment. They had travelled together in a lift then, and if she had not been quite so nervous of him she had at least been aware of his sensual attraction.

'How are you?' he enquired now, as she shifted from one foot to the other. 'I was informed you were at Oxford. Your first term is almost over, is it not? Are you enjoying it?'

Sylvie was still seeking some way to answer this without betraying the way she felt, when the lift stopped at the eighth floor and the doors slid open. Andreas stood back to allow her to precede him, and she stepped out apprehensively into the carpeted corridor, waiting with some uncertainty for him to lead the way.

Andreas, eventually, unlocked the door of a luxurious sitting room. Sylvie trod on to a pale rose carpet, patterned in blue and white, and admired half-panelled walls and long curtained windows. There were soft, expensive sofas and armchairs, tall vases of flowers, and lots of subtle lighting, to add to the room's warmth and attractiveness. Two further doors opened from the sitting room, one, she imagined, to the bathroom, and the other to his bedroom.

To her astonishment, there was a bottle of champagne resting in a bucket of ice on a trolley set with glasses, and Andreas, following her into the suite, noticed her surprise.

'I hoped you might prefer to eat here,' he remarked, without expression. 'Shall I order dinner immediately, or would you rather wait until later?'

Sylvie unbuttoned her coat, warm in the centrally-heated apartment. 'Oh, I'm in no hurry,' she admitted, unable to think of food right now, and with an inclination of his head Andreas crossed to the trolley.

'Some champagne, then,' he suggested crisply, expertly handling the cork. It popped with satisfactory effervescence, and he filled one of the tall-stemmed glasses.

Sylvie faltered over whether to take the glass or remove her coat, and setting the glass down again, Andreas courteously lifted the sheepskin from her shoulders. His dark eyes betrayed no emotion as he glimpsed her narrow shoulders, without the concealing fur, and he handed her her glass silently, after folding the coat over a chair.

He poured himself some champagne, then came back to where she was standing, raising his glass towards her. 'To education,' he declared, with sudden harshness, and she touched her glass to his and drank without saying a word.

'So——' He looked down at her without compassion, touching her shoulder with a scornful finger. 'Is this the result of some ridiculous slimming diet you have been following?' He shook his head impatiently. 'What is this foolish desire you have to look all bones?'

Sylvie caught her breath. 'I—I haven't been slimming,' she denied unsteadily. 'I—I haven't done anything. I've just lost weight, that's all.'

Andreas's dark eyes narrowed. 'Why?'

'Why?' Sylvie was confused.

'Yes, why?' he insisted roughly. 'Do they not feed you at this university?'

'Of course they feed me.' Sylvie moved her shoulders. 'The meals are very good really——'

'Then why are you so thin?' he demanded. '*Theé mou! Mitera*, you are not ill?'

'No!' Sylvie swallowed convulsively. If she had imagined their conversation at all, she had imagined nothing like this, and his reasons for interrogating her in this way could not be encouraging. 'People do—lose weight from time to time, you know. I'm sorry if you think I look a mess——'

'I did not say that,' he retorted, finishing his champagne and putting down his glass with suppressed violence. 'I was merely—concerned about you, that is all. Forget it!'

Sylvie put down her glass, too, feeling hopelessly out of her depth, and Andreas unbuttoned his jacket and ran a hand round the back of his neck. Feeling obliged to say something, Sylvie chose the only subject she could think of that might ease the situation.

'How—how is Leon?' she asked nervously. 'And—and Nikos? Does—does he still remember me?'

'Who? Leon or Nikos?' asked Andreas brusquely, and Sylvie realised he had not forgiven her for her friendship with his brother.

'Nikos, of course,' she answered now, refusing to allow him to disconcert her again. 'I—we heard from Margot that they'd returned to Alasyia, and I just wondered if he'd settled down again.'

'Nikos is fine,' replied Andreas shortly, inhaling deeply. 'And Leon, as Margot probably told you, is almost ready to return to work. The operation was a complete success.'

'I'm so glad.' Sylvie was fervent. 'He's a nice man.'

'And I am not?' suggested Andreas tautly, expelling his breath heavily, and Sylvie sighed.

'Now you're putting words into my mouth,' she declared, striving for lightness, but the dark anger in his eyes doused her attempt at levity.

'You left without telling me that you were doing so,' he said suddenly, harsh and aggressive. 'Why?'

'Why?' Sylvie gasped. 'Why, you left before I did. And you didn't tell me.'

Andreas's mouth compressed. 'That was different. You must have known I would return.'

Sylvie could hardly speak. 'I—I didn't know any such thing. How could I? The night before you left, you didn't even speak to me.'

Andreas's breathing was shallow. 'Eleni was with me,'

he declared, as if that was explanation enough, and Sylvie stared at him, shaken by his arrogance.

'Yes,' she said tremulously. 'Yes, she was. Perhaps you should remember that.'

'Oh, yes?'

'Yes.' Sylvie stumbled on. 'You were going to marry her, remember? You may have done so for all I know. Margot never mentions you in her letters.'

'I am not married,' he retorted heavily. 'Not yet.' He paused. 'Would it have meant anything to you if I had been?'

Sylvie's lips fell apart. 'I—well, I—of course it would have meant something to me. I mean——' she shifted uneasily, 'I should have congratulated you——'

'Would you? Would you really?' Andreas took a step nearer to her, and to add to the sense of panic that had gripped her at his sudden nearness, he put out his hand and ran his fingers lightly down her neck and over the prickling skin of her shoulder.

When he withdrew his hand again he did not step away, but remained where he was, only inches away from her, the palpitating rise and fall of her breasts almost brushing against his velvet waistcoat.

'Tell me about Oxford,' he said, with an abrupt change of mood. 'Are you happy there? Are you working hard?'

Sylvie's nerves were almost at screaming pitch, and she pressed her palms to her sides as she endeavoured to reply. She so much wanted to touch him, to slide her arms around his waist and press her face against his chest. But instead she had to answer him, and her voice shook ignominiously as she struggled for control.

'Ox—Oxford is very nice,' she stammered in a low tone. 'The—the people are kind and—and I've made some friends.'

'Male?' he demanded, and she gave a little shrug.

'Both sexes,' she admitted. 'No one in particular. Just fellow students—first years, like me.'

'And you are happy,' he declared flatly. 'This is what you want to do?'

Sylvie gulped. 'Does it matter?'

'Yes.' Andreas's voice had deepened. 'Yes, it matters.'

Sylvie shook her head. 'Oh, Andreas——' She could keep up the pretence no longer. 'I'm so *miserable*! I wish I was dead!'

'*Sylvie!*' Hard fingers turned her face up to his, and she blinked in the sudden violence of his gaze. 'What are you saying? That I am making you unhappy?'

'*No!*' With a little cry she abandoned all attempts to remain calm and controlled. Almost convulsively she wrapped her arms around him, pressing herself against him with a total lack of decorum. 'Oh, Andreas, I've missed you so,' she breathed huskily, and then was silenced by the satisfying possession of his mouth on hers.

It was months since he had kissed her, months since that afternoon on the yacht, when he had so nearly taken her innocence, and there was a desperate hunger in his embrace. One hand was behind her head holding her mouth to his as if he would never let her go, while the other moved restlessly against her spine, arching her hips against him, moulding her softness to the length of his body. If she had had any lingering doubts that he might not find her pale fragility distrubing, they were quickly eased. The eager passion in his kiss revealed his urgent need of her, and she abandoned herself to his lovemaking with all the fervent ardour of her nature.

'Sylvie, Sylvie,' he groaned at last, releasing her mouth to press his face into the hollow of her neck. 'I am never— *never* going to let you leave me again. I could not stand it!'

Sylvie drew back to look into his dark ravaged face.

'Do you mean that?' she whispered, and he nodded his head.

'I mean it,' he declared thickly, pulling out the pins so that her hair tumbled silkily about her shoulders. 'I do not care what anyone says. I do not care what I promised Leon. I have to have you, Sylvie. You are mine. And no one can deny that I have been very patient.'

Sylvie trembled, but something he had said troubled her. 'Leon—Leon told you that I—that I cared about you?'

'*Ti?*' He looked confused. 'Told me? Told me what? I told him. Have I not just said so?'

Sylvie blinked. 'I don't understand.'

'It is very simple,' he said huskily, taking her face between his hands. 'I went to see Leon, no? Perhaps three weeks ago. I needed to talk to someone, and he seemed the only person I could trust to be absolutely honest with me.' He paused. 'He does care about you, you know.'

'I know.' Sylvie moistened her lips. 'But what did you want to talk to him about?'

Andreas's mouth curled sensuously. 'You know, of course. *You!* The way I felt about you. What else?'

Sylvie stared at him. 'You spoke to Leon about me?'

Andreas bent his head to touch the corner of her mouth with his tongue. 'Do not pretend you are surprised, *kardhia mou*. Not now.'

Sylvie shook her head. 'You told him—you cared about me?'

'I told him I loved you,' replied Andreas huskily. 'I do, very much.'

'Oh, Andreas——' With a little sob, she wound her arms around his neck, covering his face with kisses, and by the time he had returned the compliment she was flushed and breathless.

'You believe me now?' he demanded unsteadily, and

she nodded her head half incredulously.

'But what else did you say to Leon?'

Andreas sighed. 'You are so young——'

'I am not so young. Actually,' Sylvie took a quick breath, 'I feel as if I've aged considerably these last months.'

Andreas frowned. 'The weight you have lost—you cannot mean——'

'Can't I?' Sylvie looked up at him tremulously. 'I thought I was never going to see you again.'

'Oh, Sylvie!' With a sound of anguish, he slid both arms right round her, holding her in a suffocating embrace. 'And I was convinced you would forget all about me once you were back with people of your own age.'

When he finally drew back, his eyes were disturbingly caressing, enveloping her in their warm possession. 'Leon warned me not to try and persuade you,' he said with rough emotion. 'But at least this time he did not try to stop me from coming here.'

'No. No, he wouldn't.' Sylvie made a sound of husky amusement, and Andreas frowned.

'Why not?'

'Oh——' Sylvie shook her head, 'I—I suppose because he already knew how I felt.'

'He *knew*!'

Sylvie nodded. 'He guessed.' She paused. 'After you left the island, I—well, I suppose I was pretty miserable. Leon found out why.'

Andreas uttered an oath. 'And he did not tell me!'

'I asked him not to,' explained Sylvie hastily. 'Darling, I never dreamed——'

'Say that again,' Andreas interrupted her hoarsely, and she broke off obediently.

'What?' Her lips curved. 'Darling?' She gazed at him adoringly. 'Oh, darling Andreas, I do love you!'

He was not proof against such endearments, and his mouth sought hers again, warm and persuasive. His fingers were tangled in her hair, holding her a willing prisoner, and she opened the buttons of his waistcoat to press herself nearer the heat of his body. With a muffled exclamation he thrust off his jacket and the waistcoat, and the clean masculine scent of his body assailed her, warm and male and disturbing. With consummate ease he disposed of the straps of her dress, but before propelling the zip downwards he looked into her eyes.

'You know what I want, do you not?' he demanded, half roughly, his control balanced on a knife edge. 'I want you, Sylvie. I want us to be together. Is it a very terrifying proposition?'

Sylvie wound her arms around his neck. 'Would you think I was terribly forward if I told you it was what I wanted, too?' she breathed, and he swung her off her feet and into his arms.

'I would think it sounded like heaven,' he retorted emotively, and her lips parted to accommodate his. 'Perhaps I am selfish, Sylvie. Perhaps I should respect your youth. But God knows, I need you, and I am going to teach you to need me.'

His bed was very soft and luxurious, the sheets silky smooth against Sylvie's bare skin. She knew a momentary panic after Andreas removed the rest of his clothes and came down on the bed beside her, but he was the man she loved, the man she would willingly spend the rest of her life with, if that was what he wanted, and she only wanted to make him happy.

Her ideas of the act of love were hazy, compounded of things she had heard and read, the sometimes sordid interpretations of a writer's imagination. Making love was not like that. It was a ritual act of giving and receiving, and although she was apprehensive that she would make a fool of herself, Andreas was too experienced to allow that to happen.

He did not join her on the bed and immediately demand entrance to her body as she had half expected. Instead, he started to kiss her, her eyelids, her nose, her ears and her throat, finding all the little pulses she had not known she possessed, and bringing them insistently to alert and palpitating life. Then his lips moved down, over her throat and the upturned curve of her breasts to the smooth flatness of her stomach, and the unexpectedly sensitive skin of her navel.

While he kissed her, Sylvie was becoming increasingly aware of other sensations, a kind of aching pain inside her, and a drenching sweetness that began and for which there seemed no assuagement. Then, just as her breathing was quickening, he took possession of her mouth—and her body.

It was some time before Andreas lifted his head from her shoulder, but his eyes were lazily indulgent as he surveyed her flushed face. 'Well?' he murmured, turning his lips against her skin. 'Do you forgive me for taking your virginity?'

Sylvie's lips parted. 'There's nothing to forgive. Oh, Andreas, am I terribly wanton? Did I behave badly?'

'You were sensational,' he told her huskily, amusement lurking at the corners of his mouth, and she gave him a worried look.

'So why are you smiling?' she demanded, realising belatedly that she hadn't a stitch covering her, and Andreas drew her close as he pressed his lips to her ear.

'My darling, I am smiling because I am so fortunate to be the man to awaken you.' He looked into her eyes. 'I adore you. You are everything I dreamed you would be, and more besides.'

'You mean that?' Sylvie propped herself up on her elbows.

'I mean it,' he told her huskily. 'I have never had a more satisfying experience.' His eyes darkened. 'Did I hurt you very badly?'

'Just a little,' she admitted shyly. 'But—but don't go away.' This as he would have moved away from her. 'Not yet, Andreas. Not yet.'

It was as well that Sylvie had not told her mother of her visit to London, and her proposed dinner with Andreas. She had planned to spend the night at Wimbledon, but she had intended arriving unannounced, thus providing her mother with no reason to worry if she was late.

In the event, she spent the night with Andreas, and at one o'clock in the morning they were sitting on the floor in his bedroom, eating cold chicken and salad, and drinking champagne.

'Are you happy?' he asked her, his eyes caressing, and Sylvie vigorously nodded her head.

'I can hardly believe it,' she admitted. 'I—I was sure Eleni——'

'I never loved Eleni,' Andreas assured her seriously. 'Oh, we were friends, yes, and I will admit several years ago, it was not a totally platonic relationship.'

He was watching her as he said this, but Sylvie's averted face prevented him from seeing her reaction, and with an impatient gesture, he went on:

'I never wanted to marry her, if that is what you are thinking. I had plenty of opportunity, before Giorgios Frederiks came on the scene, but I suppose I was too selfish to make the commitment.'

'Selfish?' Sylvie looked up, her eyes guarded.

'Well? What would you call it?' he countered shortly. 'She knew this. That is why she married Giorgios.'

Sylvie hesitated, her teeth digging into her lower lip. 'But you didn't marry anyone else.'

'No.' Andreas shrugged. 'Marriage has never been high on my list of priorities. Much to my parents' regret.'

Sylvie bent her head. 'Thank you for telling me.'

Andreas sighed, and put down the chicken leg he had been eating, wiping his hands on a napkin. 'Since I met you again—since you came to Athens, there has been no one else. You know what I mean.'

'I know.' Sylvie's lips tilted. 'I'm glad.'

'How could there be?' he demanded huskily. 'I have been able to think of no one else but you, and believe me, it has been hell at times.'

'Hell?'

'Yes, hell,' he muttered vehemently. 'You were so young, so innocent! While I—I was a man who was old enough to know better.'

'Andreas——'

'No, listen a moment. When you went to Monastiros with Leon, I was as jealous as any husband has a right to be! It made no difference that Leon was my brother, that he was sick, and a married man. I could not stand it, so I came to see you. And what did I find? You two holding hands on the terrace, like two lovers on honeymoon together. I was incensed. I behaved badly. But I could not bear to watch you, knowing I could not sleep nights for wanting you.'

Sylvie's cheeks were burning now, and she shook her head helplessly. 'You seemed to blame me . . .'

'I did.' His lips twisted wryly. 'For making me want you. I was too blind to realise it was more than that. That was why I took you to Stavira. I wanted to prove to myself that you were not under my skin. How wrong I was!' He grimaced.

'But when Eleni came, you went away.'

'I had to. Believe it or not, but I still possessed some sense of decency. I knew I could not tell you how I felt while Eleni was there, so I took her back to Athens, with every intention of coming back.'

'But you didn't come back,' she protested.

'Not immediately, no.' He sighed. 'As soon as my father learned I had been into my office to see if there were any urgent messages, he sent for me, and I spent the following two weeks in Tokyo, finalising a grain contract.' He shook his head. 'By the time I got back to Monastiros you had gone.'

Sylvie arched her brows. 'So what did you do?'

'I did not stay long.' He compressed his lips. 'Margot was there, and I had nothing to say to her. However,' he paused, 'I did have a conversation with Leon, which might interest you.'

'Yes?'

'Yes,' Andreas nodded. 'I told him I was going to London, to see you, and he advised me not to.'

'What?' Sylvie gasped.

'It is true.' Andreas inclined his head. 'I wanted to see you. I wanted to tell you how I felt. Leon said it would not be fair for me to interfere with your life. He said you were going to the university, that I had no right to try and prevent that. He told me to wait.'

'And you did.'

'After some argument, yes.' Andreas's tone was dry. 'He made me see I was being selfish again, that I was not giving you a chance to think for yourself. That was why I went to see him again a few weeks ago.'

Sylvie caught her breath. 'I'm so glad you did.'

'So am I,' he agreed huskily. 'Although I have to confess that I regret the months we have wasted. But perhaps he was right. Perhaps if you had not taken up your university career, you would have always wondered.'

Sylvie acknowledged the logic of this argument, but she couldn't help thinking how terrible it would have been if Andreas had not been so tenacious.

'So we will get married in two weeks,' he declared now, and Sylvie, still flushed and vibrant, as much from his lovemaking as from the shower they had taken together, gazed at him incredulously.

'You—you want to marry me?' she whispered, looking at him over the rim of her champagne glass. 'I mean,' she qualified tremulously, 'you—you don't *have* to. Just because——'

She did not finish the sentence. Andreas, dark and disturbing in the cream silk pyjama trousers which matched the jacket she was wearing, grasped her by the shoulders and hauled her up against him.

'The champagne!' she wailed anxiously, as the glass was knocked from her hand, but her anxiety turned to delight as he bore her back against the soft carpet, imprisoning her face between his palms.

'What are you talking about?' he demanded, anger vying with the suspicion that she could not be serious. 'Do you not wish to be my wife?'

'Oh, yes,' she breathed, unable to lie to him. 'I wish to be your wife, darling. I want to marry you, I want to live with you, and have your babies—I only thought——'

The searching invasion of his mouth turned her eager confession into a yielding supplication, her parting lips an invitation he could not resist. 'Yes,' he said breathlessly, when shortage of air caused them to separate, 'we will be married. I want you to wear my ring, and bear my children. But not yet. Not until I have had some time to have you all to myself.' He paused. 'You see, I *am* selfish. So tell me where you would like to spend our honeymoon?'

Sylvie linked her arms around his neck. 'Will your father allow you to get away for a honeymoon?'

Andreas smiled. 'I think so. Now that Leon has recovered, he can take over from me for a couple of months. I believe Fiji is nice at this time of the year.'

'Oh, darling,' Sylvie shook her head disbelievingly, 'what will your mother say?'

Andreas shrugged. 'She will be shocked to begin with, no doubt. But she will come round, once she sees how happy we are.'

Sylvie expelled her breath unsteadily. 'I love you.'

'And I love you,' he responded, sliding his arms beneath her and lifting her up. 'Shall we go to bed?'

'I like the way you say that,' she agreed contentedly. 'Hmm—getting married in two weeks—does that mean I shall have to go and stay with Mummy in Wimbledon until then?'

'Not if I have anything to do with it,' he retorted, getting to his feet, and Sylvie gurgled with laughter.

'Oh, good!' she said, with feeling.

Harlequin Plus

THE CYCLADIC ISLANDS

Midwinter blues, the pressures of a job or just plain
wanderlust turn many a fancy toward thoughts of
sun-kissed islands in a turquoise sea. And the perfect
answer to just such a wish is the Cyclades, a chain of small
rocky Greek islands in the Aegean Sea, which lie
southeast of Athens and north of Crete.

There is probably nothing to equal a cruise among the
Cyclades. As crafts wind their way over the incredible
blue waters of the Aegean, their passengers cannot help
but be amazed at the beauty and individuality of each
Cycladic island.

Besides varying in size and color, each island has a
distinctive aura. For instance, Delos is an island of
mystery, the home of haunting ruins that invite speculation
about a civilization of long ago...whereas a stop at the
popular island of Mykonos will bring visitors back to the
present. Bustling with delightful boutiques, filled with
tourists of every nationality, replete with lively quayside
taverns, Mykonos has truly been caught up in modern
civilization—though it still retains the charm of a simpler
past.

Yet, as individual as each island in the Cyclades group
may seem, anyone fortunate enough to travel among them
would agree that they share a few characteristics in
common: shimmering sunlight, jewellike waters...and a
glimpse of times gone by meshing with the colorful
present.

SUPERROMANCE

Longer, exciting, sensual and dramatic!

Fascinating love stories that will hold
you in their magical spell till the last page
is turned!

Now's your chance to discover the earlier
books in this exciting series. Choose from
the great selection on the following page!